KASCIUS

The K9 Files, Book 20

Dale Mayer

KASCIUS: THE K9 FILES, BOOK 20
Beverly Dale Mayer
Valley Publishing Ltd.

Copyright © 2023

All rights reserved. Except for use in any review, the reproduction or utilization of this work in whole or in part by any electronic, mechanical or other means, now known or hereafter invented, including xerography, photocopying and recording, or in any information storage or retrieval system, is forbidden without the written permission of the publisher.

This is a work of fiction. Names, characters, places, brands, media, and incidents are either the product of the author's imagination or are used fictitiously. Any resemblance to actual events, locales, or persons, living or dead, is entirely coincidental.

ISBN-13: 978-1-773367-50-7
Print Edition

Books in This Series

Ethan, Book 1
Pierce, Book 2
Zane, Book 3
Blaze, Book 4
Lucas, Book 5
Parker, Book 6
Carter, Book 7
Weston, Book 8
Greyson, Book 9
Rowan, Book 10
Caleb, Book 11
Kurt, Book 12
Tucker, Book 13
Harley, Book 14
Kyron, Book 15
Jenner, Book 16
Rhys, Book 17
Landon, Book 18
Harper, Book 19
Kascius, Book 20
Declan, Book 21
The K9 Files, Books 1–2
The K9 Files, Books 3–4
The K9 Files, Books 5–6
The K9 Files, Books 7–8
The K9 Files, Books 9–10
The K9 Files, Books 11–12

About This Book

Welcome to the all new K9 Files series reconnecting readers with the unforgettable men from SEALs of Steel in a new series of action packed, page turning romantic suspense that fans have come to expect from USA TODAY Bestselling author Dale Mayer. Pssst… you'll meet other favorite characters from SEALs of Honor and Heroes for Hire too!

An overseas trip is a great idea, especially to rescue American War Dog. When Badger tags Kascius for this job, he wants to visit his brother in Scotland at all costs—almost. Yet, at the same time, Kascius never wants to see the woman who he used to love. Arriving home for the first time in five years is a challenge, but nothing has changed. Liam, his middle brother, is warm, caring and still in love with the farm, and his younger brother, Angus, appears to still be a lightweight. Kascius can say nothing good about his relationship with his mother. But Ainsley? Now she's a different story. She's still the same beautiful woman he left behind.

Ainsley hopes seeing Kascius again can help heal the rift that still stops her from moving forward in life. She'd been in a bad place back then and still regrets the way they split. However, finding forgiveness, although it might be possible, doesn't look likely.

Adding to the personal problems, Kascius's arrival sets off a chain reaction that leaves Ainsley under suspicion of murder, as her world implodes into a chaotic nightmare.

Between dogfighting, gambling, and murder, ... the pair have their hands full—keeping Ainsley out of prison and Kascius alive. Add in the fate of the War Dog, Beamer, on Kascius's shoulders as well ...

Sign up to be notified of all Dale's releases here!

https://geni.us/DaleNews

PROLOGUE

KAT CROWED WHEN she hung up the phone. "Wow. Harper just updated me on his two surgeries, both his facial scar and his stump, and they went way better than I expected. He's two weeks post-op and healing. I had no idea it was even possible for both his operations to be early, not delayed yet again. What are the odds of that happening again?"

"And not just his life is going well. Our business is going amazingly well too," Badger pointed out, as he looked over at her and smiled.

"It's insane, but, hey, we're almost done with that stack of files, aren't we?"

"Not likely," he noted. "It seems like the more cases we solve, the more they're willing to give us."

"That's a good thing, right?"

"Yeah, but remember. It's all without pay."

"No, I know." She frowned. "Any chance they'll cover some expenses?"

"Oh, I've asked, particularly since they want us to take on a whole lot more of these."

"It's amazing how many thousands of dogs come and go in the military, all over the armed forces," she said. "So, do you have more cases already, then?"

"I do," he stated, as he lifted a stack of files. "The question is, do we have more men?"

At that, she nodded. "I know, right? I mean, it's one thing to ask us to do more. It's another thing entirely to expect us to do it when we don't have the men available."

"That was my concern too," Badger admitted, "but you know it's not in me to say no."

She smiled. "That's one of the reasons I love you. Besides, this last one with Beauty and Beast turned out even better than I expected. And now Harper and Saffron are coming down for a week. We'll get him fitted, plus he wants to talk about doing some design work with me, like an internship."

"Yeah, did he ever tell you what he was doing?"

"He's already signing up for the courses he needs," she said, with a note of satisfaction. "You know we desperately need more people in this industry."

"We do," Badger agreed, "but he'll never be as gifted as you."

She leaned over, kissed him gently, and murmured, "You're just prejudiced."

Badger laughed out loud. "Absolutely, I am," he said, with a smile. "But it still doesn't solve the problem of what we'll do in terms of getting anybody else to help."

At that, Jager walked into the room. "Hey, great news about Harper, isn't it?" he said by way of a greeting.

"Yeah, it sure is," Badger replied. "Please tell me that you have somebody else you can pull in for this next one."

"I have a couple cousins. Not my cousins, but they're cousins," he clarified. "It's not so much that they've had much dog training experience, but they were raised with dogs and love them and have an innate way with them."

"That's good," Badger noted. "What's the deal?"

"One is at loose ends, looking for something to do to help, to be of service to the rest of the world. Kascius and Karl are cousins," he noted, "Kascius is the one who told me that he would be interested. We were working on a remodeling project, and we got to talking. He would be happy to try."

"That's good news," Badger said.

At that, a head poked around the corner, and a huge broad-chested man with a shock of auburn hair came forward, grinning. "I'm Kascius," he stated, with an air of confidence that showed his true character. "And I'm always a sucker for a lost dog story."

AT THAT, BADGER grinned. "In that case, come on in because it seems like we have absolutely no end to the lost dog stories around here. You do understand there's no pay, right? It's a volunteer deal."

"Yeah, but you cover expenses, right?" he asked, with a glance at Jager.

Badger nodded. "That we do, and, if we're lucky, we might get the government to reimburse us, though it hasn't happened yet."

Kascius laughed. "Not shocking really. So whereabouts is this dog?"

Badger hesitated and asked, "What's your background?"

"Is it the accent or the hair that gave me away? I'm from Scotland."

"Scotland, *huh*?" He grinned, pulled a folder from the bottom of the stack, and asked, "How do you feel about going home for a bit?"

"I was planning on going home anyway, just hadn't made any concrete plans," he replied easily. "Why? You don't have a lost War Dog in Scotland, do you?"

"We do, indeed. It was adopted, and then the family relocated to Scotland."

"That sounds normal enough. What's the problem then?"

"It turns out that the dog didn't arrive. Well, it arrived in Scotland just in time to get lost. The family tried but couldn't find it, though according to them, they didn't get much help. Anyway this dog hasn't shown up anywhere, so we've got a missing K9 military dog."

"Well, Jesus, how could that happen and no one see it go missing?" He stared at Badger in surprise, his mind already spinning through the puzzle. Poor dog. After a regimented lifestyle, to retirement then to ... to what? It didn't bear thinking about. He'd always been in awe of those dogs and the job they did. Always so willing and happy to serve. Too bad there weren't more people like that. He already felt a kinship to the lost animal.

"That's what we don't know. You'll start with the airport and figure out where it went from there. I don't know what kind of a bond it may or may not have had with the family. We'll also see if the family is interested in taking it back, though my initial impression is an absolute no. We're short on people with the credentials to travel freely there, so you would fit the bill nicely, if you're willing."

"That's definitely me. Sure, I'll take it on. I don't suppose you have any contacts over there or any information to get me started?"

"No, I sure don't," Badger admitted. "I'll also get creative to figure out how to fund this adventure as well. But that's my problem, not yours. You're already volunteering your time."

"I've got lots of family and friends over there," he added, "so expenses shouldn't be a problem, at least once I arrive."

"Is there a sweetheart you left behind?" Badger asked, with a sideways glance at Kat.

"No, sure isn't." His voice had turned hard.

Kat looked at him, smiled, and asked, "You sure about that?"

"Sure, I'm sure. Ainsley wouldn't want anything to do with me at this point in time."

"Why is that?" she asked.

"Because I'm broken," he declared. "I served in the military there, then I migrated and joined the US military, which pissed her off pretty badly. Now that I'm no longer whole, I'm doubly certain that is the end of it."

"Sounds like she's pretty shallow, if that's the case."

"I don't think it's that so much as the fact that her brother was in the same condition, and she ended up looking after him, as his primary caregiver. She struggled trying to help him with his disabilities, and, when he died early because of his injuries, I know she held it against me that I would go into anything that would expose me to that kind of risk. So, again I don't think she'd want anything to do with nursing another broken shell all over again."

"Do you require nursing?" Badger asked.

Kascius grinned. "No, I sure don't, but you can't convince some people that you're healthy and capable of being on your own."

"Maybe she'll figure it out this time," Badger suggested.

"Maybe." Kascius shrugged, sounding unconvinced. "So when do I leave?"

"The trail's already bloody cold, since this happened two weeks ago."

Kascius stared at him in shock. "Good Lord, that dog could be anywhere by now."

"Yeah, so you better be on your way."

CHAPTER 1

EXITING THE AIRPORT, Kascius Lamond stood outside and sniffed the fresh air. The trip had been surprisingly stressful. Mostly because of the destination. He hadn't lied to Badger. He did plan to go home—sometime—but not anytime soon. This was an excuse to kill two birds with one stone.

There'd been more than enough killing in his military history, and he wanted something completely different for himself now. Like saving this dog for a start.

As he looked around, taking big gulps of fresh air and slowly rotating his neck, he realized just how long it had been since he'd been home. Now although Beamer, the War Dog he was tracking, was his primary reason to be here, the visit would involve a lot of friends and family. For the most part, that was good. Except for one, and he had no idea what he was supposed to do about her.

Except it really wasn't about Ainsley. Just something about Kat's warning that gave Kascius an idea of what Kat thought would happen, but that was BS. After Badger had shared all the details on this job with Kascius, Badger added how Kat was right. Most of their people had come away from these jobs with partners. Then Badger had corrected *most* to *all*.

Kascius wasn't against having a partner. Yet he sure as

hell was against going back to a partner he'd walked away from some five years ago. He gave his head a shake at his rampant thoughts. Better to stay focused on poor Beamer. Badger had sent the slim file to Kascius, but he hadn't had much time for more than a curious look. He'd spent a lot of time staring at the dark Malinois shepherd's face and the incredibly intelligent look in his eyes and the tilt of his head in a questioning manner. It had struck a chord in Kascius's heart. Beamer was hard to forget.

"This damn mess is already driving me crazy, and I've barely arrived." Hearing a shout off to the side, Kascius turned to see his middle brother, Liam, racing toward him. Kascius grinned. His brother hadn't aged a day. They exchanged huge bear hugs.

"My God," Liam exclaimed, looking at Kascius with a huge freckle-faced grin. "Aren't you a sight for sore eyes."

He laughed. "Damn, it's really good to see you."

"You could have come back anytime."

"Hey, I'm here now."

"And here you're staying," Liam replied immediately, slapping him on the shoulder. "I don't know what the hell made you go off and join the American army, for Christ's sake."

"Because I thought it was America, the land of milk and honey." He smiled at his brother. "I wanted to see some action. You know that better than anyone."

"*Uh-huh.*" Liam stepped back, eyeing his elder brother critically. "Now that you've seen the action, what do you think?"

"I think it sucks," Kascius admitted cheerfully, "but I'm still a better man for it."

"You're a lesser man too. Though not in any way that

matters," he added, immediately correcting course.

"Yeah. So, I got a prosthetic, and I'm missing a few teeth and a few other minor things I just might need," he replied, "but I'm not at all upset about any of that."

His brother studied him carefully and then shrugged. "As long as you aren't, I won't be either."

He laughed. "Good. Sometimes you have to be young and foolish and go off to live your dream."

"Mam is more than delighted that you're coming home."

At that, Kascius felt his throat tighten up. Yet it was a mix of worry, homesickness, and pain. "How is she?"

"She's okay. Much better now that she knows you're here," he added, with a chuckle, "but she's had a couple rough years."

"I've talked to her on the phone, but it's not the same."

"No, it sure isn't. She would never stop you from living your life, and that's been a good thing for you, but I think she's always secretly hoped you'd be coming home."

Kascius winced because Liam's understanding of Mam and her thinking was the opposite of Kascius's take on her. Plus his family didn't really know why he was coming home or that it was temporary—or that it took a job, such as this, to get him home, which was not easy to stomach. It wasn't their fault at all. Every bit of it had to do with Ainsley, which was stupid bullshit. He needed to get past that and fast.

He should never have given her that power, but why it had taken him so long to see it, he didn't know, and he was feeling worse by the minute. He looked over at his brother. "How are you doing, Liam?"

"I'm doing fine," he stated, with a bright grin. "Better than you."

"Of course, but then that's your golden life, isn't it? And the farm?"

Liam shrugged. "It's doing okay. Farming life, you know?"

"Right. Some years are good. Some are bad. Another reason why I had to get away. That wasn't the life I wanted."

"I knew that, and so did Mam ... and Dad. You had to be you."

"Yeah, I did." As they walked over to Liam's truck, Kascius eyed Liam cautiously. "Anything I should know about the family?"

"Yeah, you probably should." He stopped, ran his fingers though his hair. "If you were hoping to avoid Ainsley, that won't happen."

Kascius froze in place.

His brother gave him a knowing look. "I wondered if you were hoping to avoid her, but I might as well tell you that she's been a pretty strong mainstay in the family."

"Good God, why in the hell would that be?"

"She's a nurse now," Liam explained. "We hired her to look after Mam."

"What the hell? The last thing she ever wanted was to be around sick people." Kascius struggled to wrap his mind around the news.

Liam shrugged. "She had spent years looking after her brother, and, when she had a chance to reflect on it, I think she decided that maybe she had more to offer."

Kascius shook his head at that. That was not the Ainsley he'd left behind. "Who knew?"

His brother didn't say anything, as they got into the vehicle. Liam quickly started the engine and headed out of the airport parking area. "Will you be okay if you see her?"

Kascius snorted. "It's been a long time, why wouldn't I be?"

"That's what I'm trying to figure out, and I'm wondering if that's why you never came back."

"She's a big reason I never came back, yes."

His brother nodded. "I'm sorry she kept you away from your family."

"She was only part of the reason. Nothing quite like knowing exactly where your life is going, only to find out it's going nowhere at all."

"Right, but, at the same time, you can't blame her for that." He gave Kascius a searching look. "Or can you? I guess I don't really know what happened between the two of you."

"I don't blame her," Kascius stated, looking over at his brother, as Liam drove out of the airport traffic, heading to the family farm. "But that doesn't mean that I want to see her all the time either. Is she married?"

"She had a thing, and it looked serious." Looking at his brother, Liam hesitated, then went on. "Yet they never did get married."

Kascius felt some relief inside and then shrugged. "I'm sorry they couldn't make it work."

"Are you though?" Liam looked at him, with a slight grin.

"Listen. When I walked away, I walked away," he snapped, his voice harsher than he intended, which said much about his state of mind.

"You did, and the rest of us paid that price."

Kascius stared at his brother, not sure what to say to that.

Then Liam shrugged. "Eventually we got over it, and we all moved on with our lives. But it wasn't the same as having you around."

"Maybe not, but I couldn't stay."

"Honestly I get it, but some people might still have a few reservations about the way you went about it. I understand, but then I've got Emily in my life." He couldn't help but smile. "Nothing would tear me away from her."

At that, Kascius laughed. "You two have always been a unit. You're very lucky." He'd always wanted what they had. Had dreamed that it was possible for him and Ainsley. Only to watch it go up in flames.

"It takes time and energy."

"Of course it does. It also takes somebody giving a damn."

At that, Liam winced, followed by a heavy sigh. "I hear you there, and I'm sorry it didn't work out."

"It is what it is, but I certainly won't sit here and moan about something that happened that long ago."

"No, I wish you'd stuck around though. There was some discussion as to whether we wanted Ainsley back in our lives to that degree, but we needed somebody to look after Mam, and Ainsley's been really helpful."

"Good. I won't be staying with you guys all that long anyway. So it won't be an issue either way."

At that, Liam glanced at him. "What do you mean?"

"It's not as if I'll move in with you. I'm here for a visit only. You've got a life of your own."

"Yeah, I have a life, and, besides, as my eldest brother, you are a big part of it."

"You mean, you want me to be." Something was so comfortable about being here with Liam. They'd always been able to talk.

"Absolutely I want you to be part of it. Listen. I'm not

sure what's going on, but please don't let anything to do with Ainsley stop you from spending as much time with the family as you want to."

"I don't think that will happen."

But something in his eldest brother's voice made Liam stare at Kascius with a puzzled expression. "You mentioned something about finding a missing dog. I can't believe that, after all this time, you came all the way home for that."

"That's not what I expected either." Kascius grinned. "However, it's an American War Dog, and it was adopted by an American family, who then moved to Scotland, but the dog went missing along the way."

"But why you?" Liam shook his head, more confused than before. "I get it, that you're ..." Then he stopped.

"Not capable of serving anymore?" Kascius asked, his voice harsh, refusing to look at Liam and to see the pity on his middle brother's face.

Liam winced. "No. That's not what I meant. Look. We're bound to make a few mistakes as we try to figure out what to say and how to say it, but don't ever doubt that we love you in whatever shape you're in. We're glad to have you home."

"The shape I'm in is fine, thanks." Kascius's tone was again a bit brisker than it needed to be, and he knew it.

Liam nodded, and, after a few moments, he sighed. "Look. I'm really sorry. That didn't come out at all as I meant it. It's hard, and we'll need some time."

"It doesn't matter. I have no reason to be ashamed of anything in my life."

"Not even Mam?"

Kascius sighed. This wasn't a discussion he wanted to have. "Is she more lucid these days?"

"She is actually." When Kascius seemed surprised, Liam frowned. "I guess we didn't tell you that the new medication seems to be working, did we?"

"No, I haven't talked to her much lately, but she doesn't seem to really have much of a grasp on life."

"She does and she doesn't," Liam agreed, with a nod. "She's getting better, but you're right. She has been up and down for quite a while."

"Right," Kascius noted, "so I wasn't about to make a full-on life change for her, especially when she barely knows who I am anymore."

"She may surprise you," Liam said, with a smile.

"I hope so. It would be nice to see her, at least the version my memory has of her."

"That won't happen. She's a long way from that, even on her best day."

"*Great*." He shook his head and shrugged, wondering how difficult this trip would be.

"It's still good that you came home though. And, if you decide you don't want to stay, well, I can't say it will make me terribly happy, but I'll do my best to understand it."

He smiled at that. "Thanks, Liam. I am trying."

"That's all we can ask of anybody," he replied sadly. "Just know you're loved, and nothing else matters. None of it."

The rest of the trip was made in relative silence.

Kascius felt the odd glances coming from his brother, but it was hard for Kascius to gear up for the meeting that he knew was now imminent. A meeting he hoped to completely forget about as soon as he was out of here. As they pulled up in front of the farmhouse, he stared at it, feeling a sense of homesickness wash over him. "Wow, I'd forgotten how much it feels like home." He tried to keep his voice calm and even, but his breath caught in the back of his throat.

His brother sighed. "It'd be nice if you'd accept it as your home again."

"We'll see, but I'm not making any promises."

"No, I get it. The whole way home you've gotten stiffer and stiffer, as if you're gearing up for war."

"I am, really. Nothing like knowing that the woman you loved and who completely changed your life is right behind that door." A woman that he had hoped he would never see again.

"Maybe it's a good thing," Liam said. "Did you ever think of that?"

"Oh, I've thought about it plenty but not with any joy. Of course I didn't expect that she would be here, taking care of Mam either."

At that, Liam winced and added, "For the sake of the family, I hope you'll be—"

"What?" he interrupted. "You mean, polite?"

"It is customary. Not to say, do, act to make everybody uncomfortable, right? That might be hard, I get it, but try, will you?"

"Does she know I'm coming?"

"Yes, she does."

"Great, so she also has to know that I didn't want to come."

"That's true, but then we didn't know that you would be coming home quite so fast. You didn't give us much warning."

"No, but, hey, I might be leaving just as fast." With that, he hopped out of Liam's truck and prepared to enter his childhood home. As they walked in the front door, his sister-in-law, Emily, raced toward Kascius and threw herself into his arms, screaming with joy. He laughed, picked her up, and twirled her around in a great big hug.

When he set her back down again but held her close, he was smiling. "You're still as gorgeous as ever," he murmured. "Dang, I should have stayed at home and stolen you away from my brother."

She broke out in laughter. "If you thought you could have, you would have." She shook her head. "But there's never been anybody for me but Liam, and you know that very well."

He nodded in understanding. "That's the only reason I didn't give him a run for his money, but I still think it would have been better if I had."

She smiled. "Nah, you wanted to see him work a little harder."

"Always," he admitted, with a big grin. Then he reached down and picked her up again. "Damn, it's good to see you." When he finally set her back in place, she was beaming and flushed. When he stepped back and looked at her, his gaze widened. "What? Liam didn't say a word about this!"

She laughed. "No, he would've left that for me."

"When are you due?" Kascius asked, beaming, with merriment in his eyes.

"Four more months. We didn't tell anybody for the longest time."

He nodded. "I get that," he replied comfortably, "but you're past the danger zone this time."

"We are, yet, as far as we're concerned, we won't feel safe until we have a healthy baby in our arms. I don't think you ever feel as if you're out of the danger zone, not when you've had the number of problems I've had."

"I get it. I do. But I'm so delighted for you, after what is it? Ten years you've been together?"

"Actually make that about fourteen. You've been gone for what, seven years now?"

"More like five. At the moment, it seems as if it's only been ten minutes."

"Or closer to ten years," she suggested, with feeling. "But, as for this baby, we've been really trying for the last four or five years, and we're hoping it works out."

"It will. I'm certain of it."

She stepped back and gave him a critical once-over. "You're looking better than anticipated."

"That's good to hear." Then he quipped, "If you weren't married to that brother of mine, I'd try again."

"Nah, don't bother."

He shook his head and spoke softly. "You two always had something I was envious of, but I never could figure out how to find someone like you for myself."

She smiled at him. "It will happen in due time," she whispered, low enough that nobody else could hear.

He shook his head. "No, it's way too late for that."

She searched his face and frowned, then she stepped away, clearly ending the discussion. "Mam's been waiting to see you."

He looked at her with a tentative expression. "Will she recognize me?"

"Hard to say, but maybe she'll at least recognize your voice."

"I've tried that over the phone, but she hasn't always known who I am."

"I get that, and it's pretty rough. We see her on a day-to-day basis, whereas you're more of that voice off in the distance. Every once in a while, she says that you're coming home, and we'll sit there and wait, and by the time we ask her what she's waiting for, she's already forgotten."

"And that's a good thing, since, up until now, I never walked through the door."

"Exactly," she agreed, with a smile. "She will be delighted."

"I would love it if she recognizes me, but that's probably too much to ask for."

She nodded. "Come on. Let's get you settled in. Sorry I've kept you standing in the hallway."

He laughed as he stepped farther into the house and looked around. "I don't think you've even painted the walls in all this time."

"No, but you know how Liam feels about having a paintbrush in his hand. And me? I've never been the artistic type." He looked at her, and she shrugged. "I can bake and cook up a storm, but, when it comes to painting or anything such as that, it's not my thing."

He smiled. "What about the baby's room?"

"We've got that started at least. Definitely something we need to work on, and we haven't got there yet." Smiling shyly, she added, "It's almost as if we're afraid to jinx it."

"Depending on how my visit goes and my workload, I might take a look at that."

She looked at him. "That would be absolutely wonderful. But not knowing how it'll all work out, please don't feel that you have to."

"I may not have a choice," he replied, with a shrug. "I can only do what I can do, so we'll see how that goes."

"Perfect." She stepped farther back. "Come on in." As he walked into the living room, his youngest brother, Angus, was on the phone, but he quickly ended the call and hurried over and gave Kascius a big hug.

"Wow, here he is, the returning hero."

And, if there was a taunting edge to his voice, everybody chose to ignore it.

Kascius looked at his brother. "How you doing, baby boy?"

At that, his brother groaned. "Will I always be *baby boy* to you?"

"Yeah, you sure will," Kascius declared, with a smile. "And, if you'll make comments, then I get to make comments right back."

Angus flushed. "Fine, I get it. Save me the torture of the *baby boy* comments then."

"Save me the torture of the *hero* comments, and we'll be fine," Kascius stated, his voice not giving an inch. His baby brother Angus had always been spoiled rotten and was definitely the family favorite. Kascius had already known where he stood with the whole sibling thing and wasn't surprised at all, but still, he could push back when he needed to, then cheerfully turn and walk away.

There was always the expectation that the eldest would stay on the farm, but Kascius hadn't been half the farmer that Liam was, and so Kascius had chosen quite a different life. He didn't think anybody really understood, but, between his father's death, his mother sinking into dementia, and Ainsley being who she was, it had been more than difficult for Kascius to find a way forward in his family.

Since finding his way forward under those circumstances had been too painful, he found a way out instead.

Hearing a sudden silence and soft footsteps, he stiffened at the smirk on his baby brother's face, then turned to face

Ainsley. With a quick nod and a bright smile, Kascius greeted her. "Hey, Ainsley. How you doing?"

She looked at him steadily. "I'm doing well, thanks." But her expression was shuttered, not giving anything away.

"Good, good." He turned to look back at Emily. "Can we see Mam now?"

She looked over at Ainsley. "How's she doing?"

"She's awake but not the most lucid," she shared cautiously. "She woke up from the noise out here." She frowned at everybody. "She wanted an explanation, but I didn't tell her."

"Good," Kascius stated and walked in the direction Ainsley had come from. "In that case, let's go see her," he suggested, looking down at Emily.

At that, Emily nodded and raced forward. "Thanks, Ainsley."

Ainsley smiled but didn't shift out of the way, until Kascius stepped forward, and she realized the hallway wasn't big enough for the two of them. As if remembering how big he was, it was all she could do to squeeze past to get out of the way.

Kascius completely ignored her and kept on walking.

CHAPTER 2

AINSLEY LET OUT a slow, deep breath as she stared down the hallway where Kascius had disappeared. Liam brushed past her, almost immediately on Kascius's heels. "Thanks, Ainsley."

She nodded but didn't say anything, then walked into the kitchen and got herself a glass of water. Kascius was here now. Not some random time in the future. The realization that he was as cool and as controlled as he was had been another disturbing element. She'd never been that good at hiding her feelings, tending to wear them on her sleeve. She paid the price for that, but, in this case, it seemed to be much worse right now. She didn't even realize how bad it was, until she had seen him. The breath gushed from her chest.

"Wow, look at that," Angus said snidely from behind her. "You're almost stunned into silence."

She looked at him briefly. "Hardly." She used the same caustic tone she always reserved for him. "It was a surprise to see him, but I knew he was coming, so it's not a big deal."

"No, of course not." Angus snickered rudely.

Of all the brothers, Angus was the one she could do without. Mostly because he never let up. He never stopped bugging her, never stopped with the innuendos, and that made her very uncomfortable. He'd even asked her out a couple times. She'd gone once and had then refused to go again, realizing that no way would he ever be the man for her, and she had no intention of wasting time. Plus he made her skin crawl.

She wasn't even sure why she'd gone on that wretched date in the first place. It had brought her nothing but problems ever since. But Angus had been insistent, and she'd finally given in on a day when she'd had more than enough of Kascius and his stubbornness. But it was a day that she never forgave herself for, and she had only herself to blame.

As always, she'd been a child looking for a much bigger world than the one that she found herself in, and nothing would make her happy until she found it. Unfortunately what she found was the exact opposite of happiness, and she ended up doing something to try and make amends, knowing no amends could ever be made.

Just then Liam came back out and asked, "Did you want to go home? It occurred to me that this will push Mam's evening routine back. And will have an impact on your hours."

"It's fine," Ainsley said, with a wave of her hand. "Everybody's been waiting for him to come home."

"Oh, yeah," Angus replied, with a laugh. "*Everybody's* been waiting."

Liam shot him a disgusted look. "I'll check with Emily to see if she's okay to do the night routine. If she is, I would suggest that you take a little time for yourself and go home. Mam has been pretty demanding lately."

She nodded. "I won't say no to an evening off for a change." She gave him a grateful smile. "But only if Emily is okay with it."

He nodded and quickly disappeared. When he came

back again, he was smiling. "Good to go, Emily is totally on board."

"In that case, I'm heading home." She completely ignored Angus as she pulled on her sweater, grabbed her purse, and headed out to her car without looking back. She sat in her car for a short moment, gathering her wits, then started up the engine and pulled away, grateful that Angus hadn't run after her.

He had this habit of trying to make her look bad, making her look and feel terrible in the process. Something about him seemed to relish in other people's discomfort—as if nothing happy resided in his own soul, so he had to make everybody else around him unhappy too. She never understood it, and, the older he got, the worse he became. She didn't understand how Liam could handle it, but then, with all his farm-related duties, he didn't really have to deal with it. Everybody else was left to deal with it. Although Emily didn't have to, she was safe from all his snide remarks because of who she was. That was good for her, but it sure as hell wasn't good for anybody else in the vicinity.

Ainsley had seriously wondered at times whether she should quit this job, but she also knew that their mother didn't have too much longer to live, and Ainsley wanted to see it through. Always in the back of her mind was this thought that, maybe at some point, Kascius would come home again. Now that he had, she realized that her chances of ever having anything to do with him again were probably zero to none. She had nobody but herself to blame. Lost in her sorrow, she slowly drove home.

When she went inside her house, her sister, Sibel, looked at her and winced. "That bad, *huh?*"

She shrugged, then spoke. "Bad, but then we knew it

would be."

"Was he mean?" she asked hesitantly.

Ainsley looked at her sister, then smiled. "What do you think?"

She thought about it and shook her head. "Knowing Kascius, I suspect he was completely self-contained, almost cool."

"Exactly. There would never be anything for him to get upset about. Why would he? He walked away a long time ago."

"He walked away, yes," Sibel agreed. "Yet it's not fair to blame him for that."

"No, and I've had more than enough self-blaming all these years. Angus was his usual slimy self, and Liam was Liam, as always."

"It always amazed me that Liam could be related to the other two," Sibel noted.

"I've often wondered that myself," Ainsley admitted. "Regardless, it is what it is, but, at the same time, they're all so different."

"Of course, and which one do you prefer?" Sibel asked.

"It doesn't matter, since I made a choice that put us on different pathways."

"You don't know that." Sibel hesitated. "Did anybody mention anything about him having a partner?"

"Nobody said anything, but he did arrive alone. All I heard was something about searching for a dog, but that makes no sense, so I must have heard wrong."

"He could still be partnered up. She could be working. She could be busy. She could be doing all kinds of stuff."

"Thanks for that mental image, but I'm trying to stay positive."

"Why? You've already said you walked away."

"I haven't completely walked away," she snapped at her sister's quick grin. "I don't need you to be difficult too. I'm already struggling enough with this."

"I get that." Her sister studied her carefully. "But don't hide your feelings because you don't want to open up to something that might hurt you again."

"Why not? Self-preservation and all that?"

"Because you're hurting when he isn't here too." Sibel frowned. "And, if you're not prepared to do something about it, then you at least need to get out and need to find somebody else."

Ainsley stared at Sibel for a long moment. "That's not so easy to do."

"No, you've tried it a couple times, but I'm not sure you ever gave it a lot of effort."

"There was too much effort required in most cases, and none of that matters."

"It all matters, Ainsley. However, if you won't fight for what you really want, then you deserve to get second-best. And, hey, if you're happy with second-best, which you obviously aren't, then take a look around. There are a lot of good eligible men. But remember that second-best is just that, … second-best." With that, she walked into the kitchen to start dinner.

Ainsley knew what Sibel was trying to do, and Ainsley didn't appreciate it. Yet stopping Sibel was almost impossible. Sibel would say that Ainsley's life needed fixing, but Ainsley would say it was past fixing, that nothing was left to fix anymore.

She didn't even know if that was true or not; it's just how she felt. She didn't even know what she'd expected when she found out that Kascius was coming back. There'd been no warning, no time to prepare mentally. It was a case of hearing only yesterday that he was coming in, and suddenly there he was. But he'd always been a traveler, always somebody who wanted to go out into the world and do things.

At the time, she wanted to stay home to recover from her brother's death. She had been mentally and physically exhausted … and fed up. She thought she would be married by that time, and to find out that Kascius had been planning on doing a lot of traveling, potentially without her, had been quite disturbing. Even now that she understood that he hadn't meant without her, still, she'd had no idea that he was even contemplating joining the *United States* military, for God's sake. He had enlisted out of the blue after their last blowup, for which she took full blame, and he was gone.

She hadn't had a chance to see him or to talk to him since. Now he was such a different person that she wasn't even sure she could talk to him anymore. It wasn't that he was intimidating, but then she stopped herself. "Hell yes, he's intimidating."

He'd always been big, brawny, and tough. Somebody who could handle everything in life. Yet, at the time, she'd still been a child in so many ways. She had nobody to blame for that last blowup but herself.

Her sister called out, "Dinner is ready, if you want to eat something."

Ainsley groaned. "I'm not hungry."

Sibel poked her head around the corner. "Maybe you aren't, but that doesn't mean you shouldn't eat. You still have a job to maintain, even if it'll be a little more difficult than you thought."

She stared at her sister. "I don't understand why he had to come back now." She walked into the kitchen. "I had finally adjusted to the fact that I would never see him again."

"Maybe it's a good thing that he did come back. Maybe this time you can deal with it and then write him off permanently."

KASCIUS WOKE UP the next morning with a weird sense of strangeness. He'd checked in with Badger the night before, but—outside of seeing his mother, having a late dinner, and visiting with the family—Kascius hadn't had a chance to do anything else. But he was fully determined to change that this morning.

He quickly showered and headed to the kitchen. He knew his brother Liam would already be out on the farm. Sure enough, Emily was here, having a cup of coffee with Ainsley. He stopped, his steps faltering, as he realized she would be a mainstay in the house, then gave a mental shrug. He smiled at his sister-in-law. "How's the baby today?"

"Active." She wore a big smile as she patted her stomach. "That's a good thing."

"Absolutely." He walked over and poured himself a coffee.

Emily added, "I didn't know what you wanted to do about breakfast."

"Anything is fine, and I can make it myself, so why don't you sit there and tell me what I can have."

She laughed. "Whatever's in the fridge, feel free."

He opened the fridge, then grabbed some bacon and eggs, then turned and looked at Emily. "Have you eaten?"

"No, not really."

"So, can I make you some bacon and eggs?" Quite surprised, Emily nodded. He looked over at Ainsley. "Would you want some?"

"I have eaten, but thanks."

He nodded and proceeded to cook eggs and bacon for the two of them. He popped in some toast, and, as he was finishing, the back door opened, and his middle brother walked in.

Liam took one look at him in the kitchen and chuckled. "All those years in the war and you learned how to cook, *huh?*"

"No, all those years of living on my own, in between the years in the war." He gave his brother a grin. "How are things going out there?"

"Same old, same old," Liam replied. "Did you get any sleep?"

"Yeah, I slept well. I checked in with my bosses, and, right after breakfast, I'll be heading out."

"Okay." Liam hesitated, before adding, "It's a strange assignment, isn't it?"

"It sure is. I mostly volunteered because it would bring me back to Scotland."

"Did you need a job to come back?" Emily looked at him in horror.

"No, not at all." He laughed. "It was time."

"Absolutely it was time." She spoke with a firm note in her voice, then cast an awkward glance over at Ainsley. "We're glad to have you back."

He nodded, then placed a full plate in front of Emily. "You eat up now."

She looked at it with a chuckle. "I get that I'm supposed

to be eating for two but not for two horses."

"That's all right. Whatever is left, I'll take." And, with that, Kascius sat down, completely ignoring Ainsley, then dug into his food.

His middle brother grabbed a coffee and sat down beside him. "Any chance you can give us an idea as to what your schedule will be? Just to give us an idea if you'll be here for mealtimes?"

Kascius frowned at that, as he thought about where he was going and what he would be doing. "I can't really today, but, as soon as I get an idea of what's going on, I'll have a better idea as to what my days will look like." He thought about his mother and winced, then he turned to Ainsley. "Look. I know you can't say for sure, but is she—well, do you see her going in the next day or so?"

She stared at him, then shook her head. "You're right. I can't be certain, but I would expect her to have a little longer."

He nodded. "Good, good. I was hoping you'd say that. If something does happen, then I'll make some changes in my schedule, but hopefully she's got more days in her so that I can finish this job and then spend time with her." Although he wasn't sure what good it would do, as that first visit yesterday hadn't been great.

"I'm really glad you came back." Emily smiled. "It's been good for her."

He looked over at her and shook his head. "I don't know what planet you're on, but she didn't have the slightest idea who I was last night."

"No, but she was much less restless," Emily noted immediately. "She had a wonderful night. Better than I've seen in a while."

He looked at her. "Is it safe to say goodbye to her?"

Ainsley immediately nodded. "It would be a good idea. She has missed you terribly."

He stared at her, then shrugged. "It's hard to imagine that, when there's absolutely no understanding of whether she knows who I am or not. But I'm here now, so I'll spend as much time with her as I can." And, with that, he polished off his plate and threw back the last of his coffee and walked outside to the front, where he saw that his rental vehicle had been delivered overnight. He smiled at that, rubbing his hands. "Wheels!"

He picked up the paperwork that was under the front seat, grabbed the keys stashed down there as well, and hopped in. Before he drove anywhere, he checked the map, wondering how he would even start this mission. At the tap on his window, he looked over to see Liam standing there. "Hey. What's up?"

"You didn't say goodbye to Mam."

"Right." Kascius gave a headshake. "I looked outside to see if my vehicle came and got caught up in the paperwork."

"I get that," Liam acknowledged. "I know it's important to the women."

"I get it," he said. "Besides, I was hoping to get a coffee to go."

With that, Liam laughed. "Of course you were," he said, shaking his head with an affectionate smile.

As they walked back in, Kascius asked, "Where's Angus?"

"He went back to his place last night, and I haven't seen him yet this morning."

"Does he work on the farm with you?"

"*Pfft*, it's Angus." Liam shrugged. "So, no, he doesn't do

much work here at all."

Kascius frowned. "Is it too much for you then?" he asked his brother.

"Sometimes, sure. And now that we've got a baby coming, it could be, but that's the life of a farmer, right?"

Kascius didn't say anything to that, but his brother hadn't asked him for help, which was a good thing, since Kascius did have a job to do. That's why he was here in Scotland, and, considering that Badger had paid for the flight and the rental, Kascius could hardly bail on the job. However, he also knew things could get ugly, depending on his mother's health and what he saw for the workload here with Liam.

Kascius sighed as he walked back inside. "Let me know if I can help. Obviously I have things I must do right now with this job, but, when I get that over with, I'm not necessarily in a rush to go back home again."

At that, Liam perked up. "Seriously?"

"That's part of what I have to figure out, such as what I'm doing with my life now. I'm not exactly military material anymore."

"How is the leg?"

"It's fine," he bristled. "You don't need to worry about me in that regard. Still, I'm not sure how much help I'd be around the place."

"I never even considered that." Liam stopped, as if to collect his thoughts. "Are you capable of physical labor?"

"Yes." Kascius gave him a wave of his hand. "Lots of people survive life with a prosthetic. It's not that bad."

"Yeah, I wonder what that means to you though." Liam smiled. "You never were one to let people understand how bad things could get."

"What's the point of it? If you can't help, then all telling you does is make you worry." He walked past his brother to his mother's room.

She was asleep, but he walked in and stood for a long moment over her bed, wishing her end of life, although seemingly peaceful, could have been something full of laughter and joy.

With a heavy sigh, he walked out and headed to the kitchen, where Liam handed him a travel mug.

"Here you go. ... Fill it up. Any chance of finding out if you'll be here for dinner?"

"No clue." He looked over at Emily. "As soon as I figure it out, I'll let you know. I promise."

She smiled. "That's fine. It's not a huge deal either way." But obviously it was much more convenient for her if she did know.

"Hopefully when I get back, you'll be sound asleep and resting because, once that baby gets here, rest will be a little hard to come by."

Her face changed with the softest of smiles. "I can't wait."

He nodded, put the lid on his coffee, then bent down to give her a gentle kiss on her cheek. "Look after my nephew." And, with that, he walked out.

Almost immediately Liam raced outside behind him.

"Now what did I do?" Kascius asked him, stopping at the driver's door.

"Nephew? Do you know something I don't?"

He looked at him and frowned. "Didn't you tell me that the baby was a boy?"

"I didn't tell you anything," Liam said, immediately staring at him.

"Don't ask me. I guess I automatically assumed it was a boy."

"Well, you've certainly got Emily bewildered at the moment because we have no idea what it is."

"Perfect, then it'll be a big surprise." And, with that, he hopped into the rental truck and drove off, leaving his middle brother standing there, still staring after him. As Kascius drove, he checked the short list he had made of places to start. First was the airport. He had the cargo number documenting where Beamer had been shipped with the family.

He was still quite amazed that they had chosen to ship the War Dog all the way over here to Scotland. Some dogs traveled well, and some did not. He also wanted more background on the adoptive family involved. He'd asked Badger for that information, and it was forthcoming, but nobody had a direct line to it yet.

What Kascius didn't understand was why they would have taken on the adoption and then moved back here again. He had questions that needed answers.

How thorough had the adoption process been? What did that mean for Beamer? Did the family even care?

Kascius sure as hell did, and he'd only seen a picture of Beamer. These people had touched and hugged and fed and played and interacted with Beamer. Or at least they should have. Wouldn't their bond be tighter? Kascius shook his head.

As soon as he reached the airport, he got hold of the cargo manager dealing with live transports and spoke to him about the War Dog.

Henry was his name, and, when he realized what dog Kascius was asking about, he smiled.

"Yeah, that was one of the nicest dogs ever, but it was in rough shape in some ways. It seemed to be struggling with the cage, though it probably had a lot of cage hours. Also it had a bum hip, making it limp quite badly. There were a couple notes about injuries on Beamer, but most of the time he was great. I think they were talking about using it as a therapy animal."

"Interesting. I wondered why they would have shipped him all this way."

"Maybe they couldn't stand to part with him. I would have shipped him, if he were mine."

"I hope so, for Beamer's sake. Did you see it out of the cage?"

"I didn't personally, no. It would have been taken out to be walked by one of our handlers," Henry explained. "They also do the feeding and watering."

"Who performed those routines?"

He checked his manifest. "Says here it was Terry. He'll be coming on in about an hour, if you want to talk to him."

"Yeah, I do. I also want to see if he had any reservations about the condition of the animal."

"Sure, but I don't think he did. He was talking about him afterward in awe, about how well-behaved and how beautiful and majestic he was."

"That's good to know. I'm here checking because the animal was the property of the US military and these people adopted it."

"I did talk to some government official about it several times because, once Beamer went missing, everybody was pretty upset, especially the family."

"Were they? That's one of the things that I need to find out. How did they handle it?"

"They seemed to be quite upset. Although, now that you mention it, I don't know that it was necessarily the whole family. The young boy was definitely upset and wanted his dog back. The parents shrugged and said that it was a fact of life and maybe it wouldn't come back."

"Right, but then again that's also an adult versus a child."

"Exactly," Henry agreed. "Sometimes life works out well, and sometimes? Well, it's pretty much a shit show."

"Lord, if that isn't the truth." Kascius chuckled. "I'll walk around, take a look at where and how the animals are held, so I can get a better idea of what might have happened." With that, the two men parted ways. While waiting for the handler Terry to come on shift, Kascius examined the area, looking for entrances and exits. Just as he was about to sit and wait for Beamer's handler, Badger sent Kascius the information he had requested on the family.

As he read through it, nothing popped out at him—except that the mother was Scottish and had been trying to get back home since forever. They had applied for the War Dog adoption months and months earlier. When it came through, they had hesitated because the overseas move had come up in the meantime. However, not wanting to upset anybody, they accepted the War Dog and immediately decided they would take Beamer with them to Scotland.

When they were contacted for a routine follow-up, they apparently confessed that Beamer had gone missing on the flight. There had been no notice of anything happening before that, but Kascius also didn't get a great feeling about that. Plus, his file was too skimpy. Why hadn't the family reported the missing dog earlier? Kascius sat off to the side and phoned Beamer's adoptive owner. When Shana Melrose answered, he explained to her who he was.

"Oh," she replied, nonplussed. "I thought that had all been dealt with."

"Do you have Beamer?"

"No."

"Well then, how has it been dealt with?" An odd silence from her followed. "Did you think the US military would just forget about a missing War Dog?" he asked.

"Yeah, I did," she said wearily. "The dog is lost and has been for a couple weeks."

"Yes, but Beamer is still a very special dog, a well-trained dog who served in wars, and his case deserves due diligence."

"Right, but I don't know what I can do to help you. We did everything we could at the time, but there was no sign of it."

"Beamer is the dog's name, ma'am. Now maybe you can tell me in your own words exactly what happened."

She hesitated. "I think you should talk to my husband."

"Why is that?" Kascius asked, his suspicions immediately raised.

"Just that ..." She hesitated again.

"What's the problem, ma'am?"

She let out a slow breath. "The problem is, he went with my son to pick up the dog. When he got there, he went to use the washroom, and the dog was in the cage, but, when he came back out, the dog wasn't there anymore."

"What do you mean?"

"You heard me. I'm saying that somehow, in the time it took him to use the bathroom, the dog disappeared."

"That's hardly possible, especially at an airport with manned security and also cameras about." In fact it sounded ludicrous to Kascius.

"I get it, but I don't know what to say."

"There's an awful lot you're not saying," Kascius noted. "Did your son let Beamer go?"

The woman gasped, and then came dead silence.

"That's what happened, isn't it? Did your son take Beamer out of the crate? Did he try to take him back to the vehicle on his own or something like that?"

"I don't know. My husband won't talk about it."

"That issue is between the two of you. I'll need to talk to him, and that isn't optional. A missing War Dog should never have been overlooked for two weeks and counting. I traveled from the States on behalf of the US military to resolve the situation with this missing War Dog." She gasped again. "So, if you think this is going away, you're wrong."

"That's why you should speak to my husband."

"What about your son? I need to talk to him too."

"Do we need a lawyer?"

"I don't know," he snapped right back. "Do you?"

Just then a deep male voice came over the phone. "Hey, what's going on? What are you doing, upsetting my wife?"

"I'm here on behalf of the US military, looking for Beamer, the War Dog that you lost," Kascius snapped, his voice hard. "I understand from your wife that there's a good chance the situation wasn't as stated on the report. Sir, did your son open the cage door and let Beamer out?"

The wife was back on the phone now, as if speaking into it together. "If he did, he's not saying so, and I have no way to know either way."

"I'm looking into airport security cameras covering that area where Beamer was," Kascius stated. "Hopefully that will show us the truth."

"My son was upset," the father said.

"Upset why?"

"What I didn't realize, until that moment, is that he didn't want anything to do with the dog. He didn't want to take it with him to this new place."

"Why is that?" Kascius asked, keeping his voice unyielding.

"Because apparently, well, … he was scared of him. He thought the dog would hurt him."

"Which Beamer wouldn't have, as these dogs are highly trained and vetted. Beamer was also no longer in his prime after suffering injuries from his years of service. Plus, you had already had Beamer for how many weeks prior? Certainly enough to know that, correct?"

"Yes, but I didn't realize that my son felt as strongly as he did. So, for my son's sake, I chose not to pursue it."

"Pursue it? And what about your responsibility to the War Dog? You know perfectly well you could have contacted the US military or the adoption organization and gotten some help." He hesitated. "But you didn't want anybody to know what was going on, did you? You didn't want to be financially responsible for Beamer's expenses or be tied up in litigation over it, is that it? Tell me." When no one replied, Kascius stated, "You did sign a contract, agreeing to look after this valuable animal."

"Look. It was a tough time," he protested, "and I didn't know what to do. I thought that possibly my son may have opened the cage door in an attempt to let the dog run away. But the thing is, I wasn't gone very long. So I don't know if he could have. And we did look for the dog, but he was gone."

"Weren't you aware of your son's actions? Are you sure you didn't tell your son to open that cage door and to send

Beamer away? Or to take Beamer outside or something so that the War Dog would then disappear?" At that line of questioning, Kascius felt the ugly truth inside him. "This had nothing to do with your son not wanting Beamer. This is about *you* not wanting Beamer," Kascius snapped in disgust. "And instead of stepping up and being a man about it, you chose this route, endangering Beamer. And now you're putting the blame on your kid."

"God, look. That's not the way it happened."

The father was defensive but didn't really have much to say. At least nothing decent.

"So, it was wrong of me. What will you do? We should never have accepted that dog in the first place. When we put in the application, it seemed to be a good idea. However, when they called us and said that we could have this dog, the decision to move overseas had been made. We didn't know what to say, and we felt as if we couldn't say no at that point."

"That would have been the time to raise the issue and to tell the truth," Kascius said immediately. "You could have told them that you had changed your mind or that the circumstances had changed and that you were leaving the country. Anything would have been better than what you did." Kascius growled, as he grew more pissed. "Beamer served your country, while you stayed home. He depended on you, and you couldn't be bothered to even ensure he was safe."

"Damn, stop blaming me."

"You should have done more. Instead you've wasted everybody's time, energy, and money, and potentially put the life of this very valuable War Dog in danger," he snapped.

At that, came silence on the other end. "Look. We don't

even live in the US anymore. If you've got anything else to say, you need to contact our lawyer."

"Good," Kascius said immediately. "What's his name?"

The man's wife gasped. "Seriously, do we have to do it this way? We're not bad people. We made a mistake."

"You signed a contract with the US government, making it your responsibility to look after this War Dog. Instead of doing that, you let it go in a busy, congested area, the worst place possible for an animal such as that. You didn't give a shit about it, and you lied about it at every turn. Believe me. I'll have something to say about this in my report to the US War Department, and we'll see what they decide the punishment should be."

"You can't do anything." The man started to blather again. "We don't live there anymore."

"Yeah, and maybe we'll extradite you to come back and face charges. How's that? Now give me your lawyer's name and number." It took a few minutes, but Kascius had both. Whether either was valid would remain to be seen.

And, with that thought hanging in the air, Kascius hung up the phone. The extradition was a bluff, and he knew it, but, dammit, they had royally pissed him off. How dare they adopt a War Dog and then not follow through? Why not hand it over to somebody here? Why not contact the war department and say that they made a mistake?

Kascius sighed. Because nobody ever wanted to admit that they had made a mistake, and this father's ego was such that, even when pressed, he was quite happy to blame it on his teenage son. That pissed Kascius off even more. Swearing at that, he was surprised when someone called to him. Henry walked toward Kascius, and he frowned.

When Henry saw his face, he looked worried. "Hey,

what happened?"

"The damn father admitted that he got the son to open the crate and to let Beamer out while the father was in the bathroom. Basically thinking that, if it ever came to light, the boy wouldn't get charged. He let Beamer go because he didn't want anything to do with the War Dog anymore."

He frowned. "Seriously?"

Kascius nodded. "Just don't know why they let Beamer go at the airport, after incurring the expense of flying him overseas."

"I'll tell you exactly what it was," Henry said. "Delivery charges. They'd used a credit card that apparently they'd overcharged, so those delivery charges never went through, and they owed almost a grand on that."

"Good God," Kascius muttered. "So, they bring Beamer over and turn him loose, then don't pay the fee because, by then, the airport handlers are liable because, well, … the airport supposedly lost Beamer."

"And yet we didn't lose him obviously," Henry snapped, getting into a temper himself. "That's a really shitty thing to do."

"Yeah, on too many levels to count." Kascius blew out a hard breath. "Now I've got to figure out how to find Beamer, some two weeks later. Sometimes people are just shitty."

"What can you do, once you find Beamer? Is there anything you can do against these guys?"

"I have no idea. The guy flat-out told me that he's not even living in the same country anymore, so there's not much we could do about enforcing the contract."

At that, Henry snorted. "Isn't that so typical. They should lose their right to have another animal."

"I wonder if I could make that happen? I don't ever want to see them allowed to have another pet, but I'll have to see what the options are." He massaged the back of his neck. "So at least now we know what happened. Anyway, it would be great if we could check the security cameras, so I can get confirmation of it."

"I don't know how all that works, but I'm sure your superiors can request it."

"Yeah, I'll have them do that." Kascius pulled out his phone and sent off a text. When Badger called back right away, Kascius looked over at Henry. "That's my boss now, so I'll need a moment." He walked away from Henry and explained the scenario.

Badger snorted. "Seriously? Now that you're over the pond now too, and you make a phone call to these people, this is when they finally tell the truth? At least some of it."

"I know, right? How lame is it that the father's blaming his teenage son? I was wondering if there's any way to get the security camera footage looked at."

You think it's anything other than that?" Badger asked.

"No, I don't. I want to see if these guys did anything else or if Beamer was injured and what it took for the War Dog to leave."

"Right." Badger sighed. "You do know there won't be much I can do about it, right?"

"I'm not surprised, but it makes me so damn angry that somebody is allowed to treat a War Dog like that and get away with it."

"Yeah, I hear you," Badger agreed. "With this family in Scotland, I'll see if there's anything at the government-to-government level or maybe through some international rescue organizations or maybe Scotland's version of the

ASPCA or whatever to ensure that family never gets any animals again."

"Yeah, I wouldn't mind it at all if that could happen."

Badger added, "I'll do a first pass, dig up some possible contacts for you there. Then I'll share that with you, so you can get in touch in person, hopefully press some buttons, see what the options are, Kascius."

"Will do. And I want to check that security feed. Make sure that there's nothing else that we need to know about because now I don't trust these guys at all. Once a liar, always a liar."

"Yeah, I hear you there." Badger acknowledged. "However, again, all I can do is ask. No guarantees. We're not in the States now. Or at least, you aren't."

"Maybe the security cameras will tell us if somebody else picked up Beamer or what may have happened. I'm waiting here for the airport handler, who apparently really liked Beamer."

"Do you think it's possible he may have picked him up?"

"I don't know, but I want to check it out. And, if he did, did he keep him or did he pass him off to somebody else?"

"Jesus, poor Beamer." Badger sighed. "Retirement's not exactly anything in his wheelhouse, even with responsible humans looking after him. Beamer's had his entire life regimented up until now, then suddenly he has nothing and nobody to look after him."

"I understand how that feels too," Kascius admitted.

"Right, when we're in the military, it's everything. Then, all of a sudden, you have an injury, and you go through therapy. Suddenly you find yourself cut loose, and you don't even know what your life is supposed to be like anymore. You have to make do with what it is, but, damn, it's not an easy transition."

"Not only *not* an easy transition," Kascius murmured, "but it's also not easy learning to fend for yourself in the new world. And that's where Beamer is at too. I have to track him down." And, with that conversation over, Kascius walked back to Henry.

"So, you don't need to see my guy anymore, do you?" Henry asked.

"Yeah, I do actually. And my boss will request the airport's security tapes and see if it shows what happened to Beamer, after that family let him loose on purpose. I don't understand why the War Dog would have taken off. Unless they were the absolute worst owners ever, which, considering everything we know so far, who's to say there isn't more ugliness to find out."

"Right. Anybody who would do that to a dog, no telling what else they might have done."

"Exactly," Kascius agreed. "The other problem is, do you have any regulations here that would allow us to stop them from getting another pet, although they could already have one."

"What? So, they got rid of Beamer, only to turn around and got another dog?" Henry asked in disgust.

"It's possible. I'm not happy about it either."

"I better not see them, and believe me, I know who they are."

Kascius nodded. "As for me, I want to see these security videos, and I want to talk to Terry, Beamer's flight handler. Let's see if he has any ideas or if he might have seen Beamer afterward."

"Seen him or are you thinking he might have picked him up?"

Kascius stared at Henry. "Is that possible?"

He frowned at that. "I don't know. It's not something we've ever come up against."

"Thank God. That's the last thing we really want, isn't it?"

"Absolutely." At that, Henry looked down at his watch. "Let me go grab Terry. He should be on the clock now." With that, Henry walked away.

Kascius called after him, "Don't prep him, please."

Henry looked at him and then nodded. "Nope, I sure won't. I want to hear what he's got to say too."

At that, Kascius waited impatiently. It took about eight minutes for Henry to return with Terry, a tall and lanky kid with pimples covering his face.

Kascius studied him for a moment. "You remember Beamer, a dark Malinois shepherd that went missing here two weeks ago?"

He frowned. "No, I don't think I do."

Immediately Kascius knew the kid was lying. "The War Dog, remember? And don't bother lying to me again."

The kid flushed. "What do you mean, *again*?"

"You lied when you said you didn't know what dog I'm referring to."

Terry glanced at his supervisor, then back at Kascius. "Who are you, and what's it got to do with you?"

"I've been sent here on behalf of the US military. I represent the War Dog department, and we care about what happened to that dog."

The guy immediately flushed beet red, glanced at his boss again, and then stared down at his feet.

Kascius spoke softly but with a very specific intent. "Why don't you tell me what you did with Beamer?"

Immediately his gaze went up, then hit the floor again, trying to look anywhere but at Kascius or Henry.

"Jesus." Henry stared at the kid. "Did you take that War Dog?"

Terry shrugged. "What was I supposed to do? It was sitting here, doing nothing, and obviously nobody gave a shit about it."

Kascius spoke up again. "Yeah, so the question is, did you give a shit about it or did you just sell it to the highest bidder?"

The kid's face turned fifty shades of red and then immediately paled to white.

At that point, Henry started to swear. "Good God, Terry. You do realize that War Dog wasn't yours to do anything with and, in fact, belongs to the United States government, right? A government that cares so much about their dog that they flew this man clear over here to find it?"

Terry swallowed several times. "Look. I just… He didn't have anybody. He didn't. He needed somebody to look after him." He was frantically looking back and forth between the two of them.

"*Right*," Henry growled. "Let's not even pretend you cared about who would look after Beamer."

"So, you sold him?" Kascius asked.

Terry flushed again. "My buddy, he has dogs."

"Yeah, that's nice. So what did he want another one for?"

"He didn't say."

"Please tell me that it's not for dogfighting."

At that, the kid's eyes widened, and he staggered back slightly. "How did you know?"

"Just had a feeling, and that is the absolute worst answer

for this War Dog."

"No, no, you don't understand," the kid said eagerly. "It's a War Dog. It's trained for this."

Kascius sighed and took a deep breath. "Those dogs are slated for death, you asshole. You are talking about an injured War Dog. He's got pins in his spine and a pin in his ankle. That dog has been to hell and back, saving your country as well as ours, and this is what your sorry little ass did to Beamer?" He looked over at Henry, who still stared at the kid, looking as shocked as he was angry. "So, what can you do about this, Henry?"

"For starters, this kid is fired as of now."

Immediately Terry turned to his boss. "No, no, please, you can't. I need this job."

"Maybe you should have thought about that before you sold someone else's property that you were specifically entrusted to care for and to secure. You not only stole Beamer from here, but then you sold him knowingly to a member of a dogfighting ring, which you know full well is illegal. Jesus Christ, I still can't even fucking believe it." He walked several feet away, rubbing his hands down his face, before coming back, ever-so-slightly calmer.

Kascius stepped forward again. "Give me the name of your friend and the address."

The kid shook his head. "You don't understand. I ... I'll get in trouble."

"No, *you* don't understand, Terry. You are already in trouble," Henry snapped, pointing to a couple airport security staff members coming toward them. When Henry quickly explained what had happened, they turned and looked at the kid.

Flustered, Terry stammered, "These guys, ... like, ...

you don't understand. I mean, I know it's illegal," he admitted, shamefaced. "But I've watched them for years, so I didn't really think anything of it. These guys really get into it."

"Right, you never thought anything of it," Kascius spat. "You didn't think about the poor animals involved, did you? Or the fact that this War Dog is likely to be put in a position where he can't even defend himself, so he's what? ... Bait?"

Terry flushed. "I can call him." He pulled out his phone.

Immediately Kascius grabbed Terry's phone. "I want the number, and you're not to talk to him." Kascius addressed Henry and the two security guards. "I'm not sure how you guys feel, but if dogfighting is as illegal in your country as it is in mine, we'll want to look at taking down the entire ring."

"Definitely," replied one of the airport security guys. "We've already put a call in to our local police force here."

"Good. I want to talk to them about this."

For the next few minutes, they all stood around, waiting for the police to show up. When they did, the explanations started all over again. The minute the local authorities heard what had happened, they turned on the kid full force.

He immediately held up his hands. "I know. I know. It was stupid."

"Beyond stupid, kid," barked one of the policemen. "Now you're going down to the station to get booked. You need to produce the information on this friend of yours, including the address."

"I want to be in on this deal," Kascius noted.

The cop immediately turned and frowned, shaking his head.

"Look," Kascius explained. "I came here from the States

specifically for this War Dog. If I hadn't, you wouldn't know anything about this, so the least you can do is keep me in the loop."

"Keeping you in the loop is one thing," the officer noted, "but having you weigh in on the whole scenario? That's not possible."

Kascius frowned at him. "I'll take what I can get, but I want that War Dog, and I want Beamer alive, so we don't have any time to waste. Hopefully you can set it up so you have something decent to charge this group with—and potentially that family who adopted Beamer too."

"That we'll have to look at," the lead cop replied. "Send us the information on the family, and we'll go have a talk with them."

Kascius nodded. "I already called my boss, who has requested the video camera footage from the airport here as well. I'm interested in seeing how it all played out and how the family's teenage son got Beamer to run away."

"Right," the cop stated, shaking his head. "Jesus, can you imagine getting your kid to do that?"

"Yeah, then the father threw the kid under the bus, so he didn't blame himself, and so he would avoid paying the thousand dollar delivery fee." With that, Kascius turned and walked away.

Everybody had exchanged contact information and had been assigned tasks as to what could be done for the moment. But what Kascius needed was the address where Beamer was at. He had a general idea of the vicinity but not all of it. He stopped off to the side and waited until they hauled the kid away.

The police officer in charge walked back over to him. "Listen. I can't have you interfering in the investigation."

The statement was simple and stern.

Despite the obvious warning, Kascius chose to ignore it anyway. "That depends on how quickly you'll get to the dogfighting location. That War Dog is in no condition to fight. If you won't get Beamer out of there quickly, I'll go undercover and try to buy it. And, if that doesn't work, well, ... I guess I might just kick someone's ass to get Beamer back." He explained the fear, the urgency twisting inside him to find Beamer—before he was put in the ring to fight to the death.

Immediately he got a frown in return from the head cop.

Kascius shook his head. "Don't expect me not to do something to save this War Dog. There's probably some fight left in Beamer, but, with his wartime injuries, chances are, if he goes down, he won't get back up again. That kid Terry condemned him to his death, unless we get Beamer out of there immediately."

"The kid will pay for it, for stealing and for whatever else we can charge him with, but the dogfighting element is huge. We've been trying to put a stop to it for a long time."

"Yeah, I get that. We've got the same problem back in the States, but it still doesn't make me any happier."

The officer sighed and frowned. "Look. Come on down to the station with us, and we'll take a look at the security footage and see what else we can come up with. I've got the address where the War Dog went to, and we'll keep investigating. We've taken Terry's phone away, so he can't contact his friend. And we're checking all the other contacts in this kid's phone too. So we've got this."

"That's good to know because that friend of his needs to be taken down."

"That's the plan," the officer stated cheerfully. "And, if

you want in on it, that's all good, and we're happy to have you on the sidelines, but I can't have you in the midst of any action."

"Shit," Kascius said in disgust. "Being on the sidelines is not what I'm used to."

The cop chuckled at that. "No, I can see that. Still doesn't mean that it's not good for you every once in a while."

Kascius swore at that but agreed. "Okay, I'll meet you down at the station. I've got my truck here."

"Good enough." And, with that, the police headed out.

Immediately Henry walked over to Kascius. "Seriously? Terry, the little shit, sold Beamer to a dogfighting ring?"

"Yeah, and we need to get Beamer back fast," Kascius muttered. "Hopefully before he's dead or will need thousands of dollars in veterinary care to put him right again. I find myself wondering now if the father had anything to do with that." He looked over at Henry, who seemed confused and perplexed. "Because that would give us a hell of a reason to charge the father."

"Ah." Henry brightened. "That's something you should dig into a little further."

"I'll have to see if he's got any connections to the dog ring. That would explain why they went to all the trouble of bringing it over."

At that, Henry snorted in disgust. "Jesus, if I didn't hate that father already, you can bet I hate him now."

CHAPTER 3

KASCIUS WOKE UP too early the next morning, still adjusting to the time change and pissed off that, so far, nothing had happened in terms of the names and addresses he was supposed to get from the police. Yesterday he'd called and texted and had gone to the station. No one would talk to him. As far as he understood, when the cops had gone to the dogfighting buyer's home, it was empty, with no sign of the War Dog. Kascius wanted to track down anybody involved in the dogfighting ring, but he also had absolutely no jurisdiction to do anything here.

Kascius snorted. The cops even had the airport security cam footage and refused to show him one second of it. Still, whatever the cops saw captured on multiple airport cams had them at least believing Kascius's earlier report about the father and the son abandoning the dog at the airport. They would confirm that in an affidavit, so that the airport would, in theory, be reimbursed for those thousand dollars in transport fees regarding Beamer's overseas flight.

He shook his head, brought up Beamer's picture on his phone. As always, the image made him smile yet also pissed him off.

The whole thing was driving him crazy. As he tried to figure out what to do next, he texted Badger with an update. Badger immediately sent back a message, asking what time it was there in Scotland.

He checked his phone and groaned. **Three in the morning**, he wrote back. **And, yeah, I should be sleeping, but I'm too pissed off about what happened to Beamer to sleep.** He got up, had a quick shower, and dressed as quickly as his prosthetic allowed him to. He headed for the kitchen, intent on putting on a pot of coffee and hoping not to wake anybody up. Yet, as soon as he got there, his middle brother already sat at the kitchen table, looking a little bleary-eyed, but up and ready for whatever the day would bring.

Liam looked up. "Hey, you're up early."

"Still adjusting to time change, I think."

"Seems to me that you were always one of the early risers."

"I am." He looked over at his brother as he passed him, heading to the coffeepot. "How is Mam doing?"

"She's holding. I checked on her earlier this morning, and she was awake, of course, but she's not ready for tea yet."

"Does she get up this early?"

"She doesn't get up per se, ... and she doesn't sleep very much anymore."

"Right." Kascius opened the cupboard and reached for a mug.

"She did ask for Ainsley to come in early this morning. Mam wants a bath."

"That's a good sign that she's doing better, isn't it?" Kascius brought his full coffee mug to the table and sat.

"Maybe. I asked Mam if she wanted to see you, and she gave me a blank look, as if she didn't understand who you were."

Kascius winced at that. "Right. Such an odd feeling to

not even register in her brain."

"Don't take it personally. I'm not sure she recognized me. She looked a little off."

"Good, but off?" he asked. "I don't get it."

Liam gave him a half smile. "Yeah. It's a tricky thing. Not seeing her on a day-to-day basis, I can see how that wouldn't make sense to you. Give it a little time."

"Coffee, that's what I need," Kascius said, rotating his hot cup with a smile to his brother. "It's surprising how much it helps when it comes to understanding things that just don't make sense."

Liam chuckled. "Isn't that the truth. It's such a weird stage of life right now."

"I agree with you there, although I'm not sure we're talking about the same stages."

At that, Liam looked at him and then shrugged. "No, you're right. I guess our individual stages are quite different, but it's still the passing of an era when Mam goes, and the arrival of a new era when my child is born. I always thought our parents would be around for that."

"Of course you did. Plus, it's the first and potentially the only grandchild of the family. Isn't that something to think about?" he noted, staring at Liam.

"Yes, it sure is."

"You know, when we were growing up, it seemed we would all get married, have kids, and be together. A big happy family, you know? Then something happened, and I don't even know what it was."

"I think a family grows apart with the years," Liam suggested.

Kascius nodded. "You make a decision that has a huge impact on the rest of your world, and sometimes you stay in love with it, make peace with it, and sometimes you must get out."

"Is that what it was for you?" Liam asked him. "Was it a case of needing to get out?"

"After you were given the farm, and I became the disgraced one, it was a little hard to sit here. I had obviously overstayed my welcome."

Liam didn't even bother flinching at that. "I told Dad not to do it."

"I don't doubt that, but it doesn't matter because they did it anyway."

"Yeah, they did. I told him that they were ruining something between us and that there was no need to make it *my* farm, but they wouldn't listen."

"For all of Dad's faults, one of the worst was his anger and his stubbornness." Kascius shook his head. "Always angry."

"Something about your relationship with Dad brought the worst out of him," Liam murmured, staring at his eldest brother. "I never caught that same anger myself, although I did see it directed at you."

"You never caught it because you never bucked him. You were happy to be a farmer, to stay here, and to marry your high school sweetheart, and to do whatever Dad told you to do. That was never for me. I could never make him see that I would die here if I stayed and that I could never be what Dad wanted me to be, which was a clone of himself." He looked at Liam in awe, adding in a wry tone, "You had already filled that position in many ways. No way I could compete, and I didn't even want to try."

"No child should ever have to compete," Liam snapped. "Maybe I wasn't great at making that point clear to them, but, now that I have a child coming myself, it seems as if a lot of the mistakes I made growing up are about to come back and confront me."

At that, Kascius stared at him. "Meaning?"

"I don't even know, but, for a fact, I wasn't a great brother to you. I sure as hell tried harder with Angus, but I wasn't exactly a great brother there either."

"That's interesting. I find myself wondering what it is great brothers are supposed to do?" Kascius asked curiously.

"It wasn't your job to make peace in the family. You had to make a life for yourself, and thankfully you were happy to do what Dad wanted you to do." At that, he asked, "Or were you?"

Liam looked at him. "What?"

"Were you happy to take over the farm, or did you feel like you were pushed into it?"

"I felt as if I was pushed into it in some ways, but otherwise I was very happy about it. I was happy enough when they handed it to me on a platter, aside from the trouble it caused. Everybody wants to make their own way in the world, and I got a huge head start handed to me."

"I'll have to admit, I was surprised they cut Angus out."

"I think that's partly what Mam was trying to change," Liam added. "And I don't know how I feel about her trying to change it, after it was given to me. Operating capital is important when it comes to making this place run."

"Do you have the deed?"

"Yes, but Mam still owns part of it. Only a small part but enough that she'd stay fine until her death. She may have left the rest of it to Angus too. I don't know."

Kascius nodded. "I can see her doing that, and it probably would have been one of the few times she bucked Dad."

"They had a couple fights toward the end, and I'm pretty sure it was about the farm."

"How would you feel if you co-owned it with Angus?" Liam shot him a look at that. "Right." Kascius laughed. "About as good as I felt about taking on the entire family responsibility and looking after everybody if I got it."

At that, Liam stared at him. "What do you mean?"

"Maybe you didn't have the same stipulations that I did, but Dad made it very clear that I was expected to take on the farm, but also all of your and Angus's care and see to your education, plus care for Mam. If I took on the farm, I wasn't really given a choice about what my life would be."

"What do you mean by our care?" Liam got up and poured a second cup of coffee before slamming it on the table and dropping into his chair.

"I was supposed to give you two an income for the rest of your lives, so you didn't have to do a damn thing in this world but sit here and enjoy the fruits of my labor," Kascius said, with a wry look. "And, for Dad, he brooked absolutely no exceptions to that rule. You would never get a portion of the land, which would have made more sense to me. Angus won't get a portion of land either, and we wouldn't all share in Mam's care. As he put it, *It would be me, me, and me.* On top of that, I was expected to give up all my hopes and dreams, marry the first solid childbearing woman I could find, and continue the dynasty."

Liam sat back, his jaw dropping. "Jesus, Dad said that to you?"

"Hell, yes. On several different occasions. That was part of the reason for our huge fight. As far as I was concerned, that wasn't a good thing for any of us, and Dad didn't agree. We had one hell of a fight over it all, and you can see what happened. I lost, big-time." Kascius then laughed, but, for all his best efforts, still a twinge of bitterness filled it. "There's always a winner and a loser, and, in this case, you came out on top, even though you weren't even involved in the fight."

"Jesus," Liam repeated. "There are still times when I wish I could beat up the old man, but he's not even here to get angry at."

"Wouldn't matter if he was." Kascius shrugged. "I didn't take well to the terms, and you can bet Dad didn't take well to being told how I would live my life."

"No, of course not." Liam stared at his eldest brother, fascinated. "I suppose it all blew up at the same time."

"It sure did. Those were a rough few weeks for me."

Liam shook his head. "I didn't know any of this. ... Dad didn't tell me any of that, and he never, ever mentioned supporting everybody or even being solely responsible for Mam. Just that she got to stay here and that her piece of land rejoins the rest on her death. If she made changes in favor of Angus, I don't know. I have no idea what her will says."

"No? I suppose he wouldn't have put the same conditions on you because what if you walked away on him too? I was more than happy to help out when I could. I was more than happy to do my share, but I won't take on all that. It wasn't in my heart or my soul, and I sure didn't think it was a good thing for the rest of you either."

"He didn't put any of that on me. Not at all," Liam stated. "But you're right. If I'd had any idea that those were the conditions, I wouldn't have accepted them either."

"So, once Dad realized I was serious, and you would likely go in the same direction, Dad backed off and dropped them."

"But that's not fair," Liam exclaimed, staring at Kascius.

"Jesus, that's not fair at all."

"Dad didn't care about that. As long as we did what we were told, it was all good."

"You saw that side of him so clearly, and I didn't really even see it at all." Liam slumped in his chair. "It feels as if we had two very different childhoods."

"We did. You weren't the eldest, so you weren't expected to take over. You became the pride and joy of Dad's life when you took to farming as he did. Therefore, I think he went all in with you, and that was it. Of course you have to wonder if Angus would have turned out a little better if he'd been given a little more responsibility and a little work to do, investing in his own future."

"Jesus." Liam lifted his cup and took a big drink. "I ended up with something that shouldn't have been mine."

"That's life, brother," Kascius murmured. "I certainly don't begrudge you the farm."

"No, but maybe you should." Liam turned on Kascius. "Maybe it wouldn't have taken you quite so long to come back."

Kascius stared at his brother. "Did it really bother you that I left?"

"Hell, yes. You are my brother," he roared in exasperation. "I thought we were close, but then from one day to the next, you were gone. And not just away in another town, you weren't even in the same country. You chose to leave us to go join the military, for another country of all things. How do you think that made us feel?"

"I don't know about you guys, but Mam told me flat-out that if I didn't go along with Dad's wishes, it was better that I wasn't even under his roof."

There was silence as the two brothers sat here, drinking

coffee.

"I'm sorry," Liam said out of the blue.

Kascius looked at him, then shook his head. "I didn't tell you to make you feel bad."

"Maybe not but somebody should have told me—and a hell of a long time ago. No way Dad should have been allowed to do what he did."

"It was his farm, so what could I do?" Kascius shrugged. "And, after all that, I knew everybody was angry because I didn't come home again, but there wasn't anything here for me."

"Particularly after Angus and Ainsley, I guess, *huh?*"

"Ainsley to a certain extent, yes. She wanted what I couldn't give and doesn't want what I currently have, so it's really not an issue."

At that, his brother looked at him. "Do you still care?"

Kascius gave a half laugh. "I can't even begin to answer that question. What I am right now? … I'm not a whole man, and she fought against me ever having her heart again," he declared, with a wry look at his brother. "So you can bet I won't be going in that direction." Seeing the incomprehension on Liam's face, Kascius pointed to his prosthetic. "It's not obvious, yet it is."

Liam looked down at the prosthetic, and his expression cleared. "I don't think she's quite so shallow anymore."

"Doesn't matter whether she is or not," Kascius snapped, his voice hardening. "You can bet I won't be going back in that direction."

"Got it." Liam groaned, as he sat here. "God, I didn't even know my parents. Particularly my father."

"He was a hard-ass," Kascius stated helpfully.

At that, Liam burst out laughing. "Good God. Do you

think Angus had as many problems with Dad?"

"No, not at all," Kascius shook his head. "I'm not saying that Angus's life was easy by any means, but, with Mam always taking his side, and him being the baby—"

"Right, his childhood was quite different from either of ours."

"Yep, and still, I'm not sure it was any better." Kascius shook his head. "No way to know."

"I presume you've never talked to him about it?"

"No, I sure haven't. I find it hard enough to talk to him as it is."

"In some ways he's completely different from us. You and I were always close, which is why I was devastated when you got up and walked away."

Kascius winced. "I get that. I'm sorry. I was pretty angry, hurt at the time. I wouldn't have been much good to you anyway."

"Yeah, you would have. You were my brother, and I loved you."

"You put that in past tense," he noted, with a wry look. "Glad to know we're also capable of moving on."

Liam flushed bright red. "Sorry, I didn't even realize I did that. Over the years, when things got tough, I often thought about you being out there somewhere, fancy-free, not having any responsibilities to tie you down. I never really understood your need to go into the military or that whole *service to your country* thing. I was much more microfocused on service to the family."

"Which is why you're also the best person for the farm," Kascius said. "I don't begrudge you that. It was hard being around and having it thrown in my face all the time."

At that, Liam frowned and stared off into the distance.

"Now *that* I do remember. Bits and pieces of conversations at dinner that I didn't understand." Then he looked over at his brother. "Is that what Dad was doing?"

Kascius nodded. "Yeah. Constant reminders that I had given it all up, and it was too damn bad that I was so stubborn and so stupid that I couldn't see what was in front of me, but now I'd lost my opportunity to make good, and he'd lost his son. So it was better if I left."

"Crap, I do remember something about that, and Mam sided with him, didn't she?"

"Yep, she sure did." He looked over at his brother. "We really don't need to rehash all this, you know."

"We're not rehashing anything." Liam frowned. "It feels as if I've never heard it before. Yet, as I hear the details, I realize I have heard it all before. I just didn't understand all the nuances."

"No need to understand them at this point," Kascius noted. "An awful lot of things in life we can change, and an awful lot we can't. So, why not focus on the things we can? Dad is long gone, Mam is dying, and the farm is yours. Yeah, you'll probably end up having Angus as a co-owner on a piece of it, but maybe that's okay too."

"I can't even imagine it. Right now, the decisions are mine and mine alone, so having to deal with Angus on running the farm would be tough."

"How is the relationship between the two of you?"

"It sucks. He never works. He hasn't come around looking for money so far, but he has asked to borrow some several times."

"Have you lent it to him?"

"Hell no, and it's a sore point between us. The farm is doing okay, but it certainly isn't generating spare money for those things."

"Those things?" Kascius repeated cautiously. "What's he into? Outside of the costs of his own living?"

"I don't know. Gambling, I suspect, but I'm not certain. Of course he never says he needs money for gambling, yet he needs money all the damn time."

"Does he work at all?"

"He does somewhat, I guess. He has that business partner that he apparently does some things with, but, anytime I ask him for clear-cut answers about what his job is, I never get one."

"That's not good. I wonder what he would say if I came right out and asked him?"

"You can try. I don't have any answers for you. I want to know what he's doing, but it doesn't appear to be something that I'm privy to."

"Yet after all these years, you'd think someone would know what kind of business he's in."

"He was supposed to have gone into business when he dropped out of college." Liam gave a rueful laugh. "Mam was upset at first, but then was totally okay because it meant that he would be around more for her."

"Right, and I guess that's good if he was taking some of the pressure off Emily and helping to look after Mam then."

Liam looked at him. "Whatever did I say that gave you that impression? Angus has always been a bit of a black sheep, and he doesn't lift a finger. Not for you or me or Mam. That hasn't changed."

"Hey, I thought that was just me," Kascius said, with a laugh.

"In a lot of ways, I think I was the dutiful son, and, whether I liked it or not, I followed along because that's what was expected of me. I wasn't like you, and I guess I didn't care enough to go off and to see the world and to make my fortune or whatever that saying is. I was quite happy farming, and it seemed to suit me, but then I didn't understand the dissatisfaction everybody else seemed to have with their lives."

"Sure, but remember. We weren't handed successful income-producing farms. Angus would have needed to figure out how to make money somehow, and I would have had to go out and find a life of my own."

Liam got up abruptly and walked over to the fridge. "After all this talk, I need to eat, and then I'll go out and bury myself in this farm that apparently I got lucky on, and nobody else did."

Immediately Kascius hopped up. "Hey, look. I'm not saying that any of this shouldn't have happened. Just that it shouldn't have gone down the way it did. I don't know what our brother is even doing with his life, if anything. It's not my intention to criticize. I just know that, when you don't have a focus, you have to make one, and that doesn't always turn out the way everybody else wants it to be."

"No, you're right." Liam slammed the fridge closed. "But I've often wondered what it was that made Angus tick, and I never got an answer. I don't know what's going on in that brain of his. I do know that he makes Emily uncomfortable sometimes, and I've definitely gotten the same impression from Ainsley."

"Really? I thought they'd be married by now."

Liam looked over at him. "There was a time when we all thought that, but honestly now I'm not sure if it was because of her or because of Angus."

Kascius stared at his middle brother for a long time. "Are

you saying that Angus made it out to be more than it was?"

"I'm not sure what I'm saying," he snapped. "It would be nice if it didn't become an issue though, as we have enough issues."

"Right, I get it. There's got to be peace and quiet here. I'm sorry if my presence is disruptive, and I really am okay to go to a hotel, if that would be better."

"Emily would be heartbroken," Liam responded instantly, "and honestly so would I. There is nothing I would like better than to have you settle close by, and we could be a family, whatever family we choose to make it be. And, if you want a part of the farm, all you need to do is to tell me, and somehow I'll think how best to make that happen. … However, back in the present, you'll have to get your own breakfast. I'm too upset to eat." And, with that, Liam turned and walked out of the kitchen, leaving Kascius to stare behind him.

He had never in any way said that he wanted to be part of the farm. He didn't know where that was coming from, unless it was just guilt on his brother's part. And honestly that wasn't fair either. Liam had never been a part of the original fight, not at all.

Kascius considered all this as he cooked breakfast. He made more than enough for Liam, should he come back in a better mood shortly. Kascius kept it warming in the oven. On his third cup of coffee, Kascius could let go of their earlier conversation.

Somewhere along the line, there had to be an end to all this pain brought on by naïve actions of their father. And speaking of parents, he got up and knocked gently on his mother's door, then opened the door and smiled at her. "How are you doing this morning?" he asked gently.

She looked up at him fretfully. "Is Ainsley here yet?"

"No, not yet," Had Liam called her in early? "Do you want me to go check for you?" She immediately nodded. "And how about a cup of tea? Would you like that?"

She stared at him. "I don't know who you are, but that would be very nice."

"I am Kascius, your son. Let me go get you a cup." With a sigh, he turned and walked out. He texted Liam from the kitchen, asking if he had contacted Ainsley.

His brother texted back, saying he would do it right away.

And, with that, Kascius went back in to see his mother now sitting up, but not looking well. She was anxious, looking all over the room at anything but him. "Liam contacted Ainsley," he told Mam, walking to her bedside with her requested tea. "Are you okay? Do you need something else with your tea?"

"I need my medicine," she whispered, her voice fretful.

"I don't know what medicine you need or when you take it." She pointed to a bottle on the side, but he shook it found it was empty. He frowned. "It's empty. We'll ask Ainsley when she gets here."

She looked at him and immediately cried out, "I need my medicine. Please, I need my medicine now."

He tried to calm her down, but it wasn't happening, and she was getting more anxious by the minute. He picked up his phone and called Liam. "I need Ainsley's number."

"What's the matter?"

"Mam's really distraught and is asking for her medicine."

"Yeah, she often gets that way, when she's looking for medicine, but it should be right there."

"A bottle is here, but it's empty."

At that, his brother swore. "Look after her. I'm coming back."

"It's okay. I'll call Ainsley and see how far away she is. Then we'll get to the bottom of it. I need to get up to speed on this stuff anyway. I can update you then."

"Honestly it's probably nothing, but you can never really tell at her age."

KASCIUS'S PHONE CALL woke up Ainsley with a short recap of Mam's request and an urgent plea to come in early, long before her alarm to start her day even went off. So she arrived extra early today, waving off Kascius, so she could sit with Bella—Mam, to her family—for a while, to take stock of the situation. Yet Ainsley had a hard time accepting what she saw, what she felt. She didn't move from her seat for a good hour. Somehow she thought by sitting here that it would become clearer. Yet it didn't.

Ainsley sat beside Bella with a cup of tea for herself, long since cold, and noted a sunken look to the older woman's features today.

Then Emily walked in, smiled at Ainsley, and asked, "How is Mam?"

"She's fading," Ainsley said bluntly. "It's interesting that Kascius asked me if she would make it through the next few days because honestly she's gone downhill much faster today."

Immediately Emily cringed, and the color faded from her skin. "Oh, I was so hoping she'd make it until the baby comes."

Ainsley looked at her and then shook her head. "Yesterday I would have said possibly, but today? I'm not thinking so. I'm sorry."

"Gosh, this might be naïve, but I was hoping she would be aware enough that she could help heal the rift with Kascius," Emily murmured.

"I didn't realize there was one."

"It all went down at the same time." Emily sat down on the other chair to stare at the sleeping woman. "It was pretty rough. Something was the final impetus for Kascius to leave. Then, after that, it didn't seem as if we ever had a chance to improve things."

Ainsley didn't say anything, not knowing whether Emily was fishing for information on Ainsley's part in all this or if something else was going on.

Finally Emily sighed, then sat back and glanced at Ainsley. "I've noticed that you and Angus don't get along all that well."

Ainsley shrugged.

"Angus caused the rift with their mother," Emily shared. "Liam was always the favorite child because of the farming element. And, while that made life a little easier for Liam, it made things much harder on Kascius and Angus. Being the eldest, Kascius was expected to farm, but it wasn't his thing. So, when Liam was the one who took to it so fast and so young, he inherited the property. At that point in time, it wasn't fair to Angus or to Kascius, and it definitely caused some issues. Liam got everything, and they got nothing."

"Oh." Ainsley gasped. "I didn't realize it was just Liam's farm."

Emily sighed, looking down at her clasped hands. "Then all of a sudden, after their father's death, Mam told Angus that all of the money was to go to him because Liam got the farm. However, the trouble was, without the money, it's hard to operate the farm."

Ainsley had definitely seen that. Liam worked morning and night on the farm. "And what about Kascius?" she asked. "Did he get cut out entirely? It's not as if Angus works the farm or helps in any way. So why should he get anything more than Kascius?"

"That was the next problem. Apparently there was quite an upset between Kascius and his mother, but I never did hear what it was."

"So, are you sure that there was a quarrel between Kascius and his mother or that somebody might have *implied* there was an issue between the two of them?"

Emily considered Ainsley shrewdly, then continued. "If you're thinking what I'm thinking, I would agree with you. But we've never been able to prove it, and, of course, once Kascius found out about the whole deal, no way he would ever come back. It was such a slap in the face, as if neither parent gave a shit that he was their eldest son or not." Emily sighed. "But we could never figure out how to make him come back long enough to realize that at least some of his family loved him. We talked on the phone, texted really. Sometimes Kascius called to talk to Mam but not often, although more so since his injuries. Not that she knew who he was."

"Sure," Ainsley muttered, hurting for Kascius. She had no idea about all this. However, if it had happened around the same time that they had broken up, no wonder he'd up and left. "But you and Liam got the farm, and I think Angus got land but I'm not sure on that. I am however pretty sure Kascius thinks that nobody cares about him at all."

"That's part of the problem that we're already dealing

with." Emily waved a hand toward the sleeping woman. "I was hoping Mam would live long enough and be lucid enough to tell us what was going on."

"She is lucid sometimes. I'm not too sure what to say about all this," Ainsley said in bewilderment. "Honestly I always thought he left because of me."

"Oh, he did," Emily noted. "It was one more thing in a series of final straws. In his mind, he believed that nobody here gave a shit about him, so he just upped and left to create a new life for himself. It broke Liam's heart for a long time—and mine too—but we understood why he left. And then you hooked up with Angus, and that was more than Kascius could bear. I think that made him decide to stay away."

"I never hooked up with Angus." Ainsley struggled to swallow.

Emily looked over at her. "What? What are you talking about?"

"You heard me." Ainsley briefly closed her eyes, before turning to face Emily directly. "I was never with Angus. I went out with him one time, and that was awful enough that I swore I would never do it again in one million years. It was that bad."

Emily sat back in her chair and stared. "Oh my God. Angus told us that you loved him but was angry at him over something and that he was trying to get you back, how he loved you and wanted to marry you."

Her jaw dropped. After a mind-numbing moment to gather her wits, she cried out, "That is complete and utter BS. Angus loves himself, and that's all. End of story."

Emily laughed at that. "Wow, I wasn't sure if you understood that, but, yes, he's a self-centered little narcissist. But, at no point in time did we ever see anything other than what

Angus told us."

"He's a liar and a cheat," Ainsley said hotly. "I think it's disgusting that Kascius would get cut out of the will. He already felt as if his father hated his guts because he wasn't into farming, and that hurt him terribly. I remember when that happened. He didn't blame Liam for it—or you of course—but Kascius sure as hell didn't want anything to do with his father after that."

"Ah, particularly when his father made it very clear that he didn't want anything to do with Kascius," Emily added. "Either you were a farmer or you were nothing around here. Unless you were the baby. Kascius couldn't fill that spot either, so nothing was here for him. Particularly after the two of you had that big breakup," Emily added, studying Ainsley. "We never quite understood what happened with that."

"It doesn't matter." Ainsley groaned. "I was an idiot. I was a stupid child, still emotionally overwrought after my brother's death, and said some things I shouldn't have. Kascius was upset and took off. I expected him to come back, but he didn't. And you know how that goes. I said something. He said something, and, the next thing I knew, it was a huge mess. Then I went out on that one date with Angus, a decision I regret to this day. I swear to God he must have said something to Kascius about it because, the next thing I knew, Kascius was gone. Not a word goodbye. Never to return."

"And now that he's back?"

"You saw how he looked at me. I'm less than nothing to him." Ainsley wrapped her arms around her chest, not even sure what to think or to feel, and, damn it, if the tears didn't start to choke her up. She brushed them away. "I've regretted so much in my life. I need to stop feeding these regrets with any more energy. I need to find a way to get out of this rut and to have a new life. A life I can actually live."

"If you figure out how to do that, let us know," Emily whispered. "If you're right, and, you seem to be, you'll be out of a job soon."

Ainsley stared at her friend. "I didn't even think of that." She turned to stare down at the sleeping Bella. "Good God. Who wants a job where it only ends when your patient dies?" She sighed. "You know I care about her, right?"

"You've always been close to her," Emily agreed. "It's one of the reasons that we hired you because we knew that it would make her happy. Even with all the sibling issues, we've only wanted what was best for her."

"But now I'm struggling with what you told me—because if Bella treated Kascius like that?"

"We can't blame her any more than you can blame the rest of us. We have our feelings, and we have our preferences, and it seems nobody gives a shit about fairness."

"I don't get that," Ainsley whispered. "I really don't."

"No, and that's because you're one of the nice people in the world." Emily smiled at her.

"Maybe, but there's no joy in being one of the nice people," she murmured. "Remember? The nice people are the ones who end up last or whatever that saying is."

"It depends on whether it's something you want to be first for. In this case it doesn't sound as if you particularly care."

"Oh, I care, but I made a lot of mistakes, and I certainly haven't found anybody to replace Kascius, but now? ... Now that I see how he looks at me, I will find someone else. So, if nothing else, his coming home has been good for me, to clear the air and to get my own priorities straight."

"I wouldn't rush it because the priorities in your mind are probably not the same priorities that I see."

"What do you mean?" Ainsley raised her eyebrows.

"You saw indifference. I saw an *attempt* at indifference that failed miserably."

She stared at her. "What does that mean?"

"Kascius was not indifferent to your presence at all," Emily explained, leaning forward and patting her friend's knees. "Kascius was struggling to appear completely normal and natural, and he did a good job of it, but it was obvious that he was hurting."

"That's BS. If he cared, he would have done something over the last few years."

"Maybe, maybe not. Judge him all you want, but, if you don't ask him or don't get to the bottom of it, you have no idea what really happened. With all these issues, plus God only knows what Angus told him, we can't really know what all went down or why Kascius chose to stay away. When you think about all the things that faced him if he returned, you can imagine why he turned his back on it all and stayed away."

"Until now." Ainsley smiled. "To think that he came back for a War Dog? Who would have thought that would be the reason?"

"But that wasn't the only reason, so it was good to come back and to see how things are. He wanted to see his mother, and, considering how she has treated him, I think that may be more than she deserves in some ways. I don't hold anything against her. She's a product of her generation, but she was never, ever easy on Kascius. She never gave him the slightest bit of leniency. Yet still, to him, she was his mother.

"Once he bucked his father, that was it in his parents'

eyes. If you did anything against Kascius's father, good luck trying to have a life afterward. Honestly, Kascius's only choice was to leave the farm, but he didn't have to leave the country. That part he did willfully, perhaps to get away, maybe to hurt the rest of the family. But, in the end, I think all he ended up doing was hurting himself."

"I don't know about hurting himself," Ainsley said, "because—didn't you see? He came back one hell of a man. It might have hurt him to leave, but it was the making of him in so many ways."

At that, Emily chuckled. "Yeah, if nothing else, he was always a big man. A man who turned heads. Yet now, as you say, he's a hell of a man, and no way you can ignore that commanding presence when he walks into a room. I'm really glad he's on our side, whatever side that is."

"Do we need sides now?" Ainsley asked, with a wry note of humor. "Because, if we do, I think I'm on the wrong side. That was a long time ago, but I know it hasn't changed."

"I'm pretty sure he thinks you don't want anything to do with him."

"Why is that?"

Emily looked over at her friend and smiled. "Because of something that you always told us and him, something that he took to heart."

"What's that?"

"You really didn't even notice it, did you?"

"Notice what?"

Emily shook her head. "I won't tell you. That is something you'll have to figure out for yourself. It feels disloyal to say any more than that."

"And yet you're leaving me hanging." She stared at Emily in frustration. "That doesn't feel fair either."

"No, but think about all the reasons why you didn't want anything to do with Kascius all those years ago, and then apply it to the person he is today, and maybe you'll come up with the same answers that I did. One thing I do know is this. He deserves somebody who'll be there for him 100 percent. He's been shafted by this family, time and time again, and that's the last thing he needs any more of. Betrayal at that level always hurts, but, when it's family, it hurts so much more."

"That sounds very cryptic." Ainsley started to get angry. "Are you serious that I have to figure it out on my own?"

"I am. I think the value of figuring it out on your own will be worth a lot more than me just telling you."

Emily's wording just made it worse for Ainsley, who replied, "Yeah, well, maybe that isn't for you to say. It sounds right now as if you're making this much harder on me than it needs to be. This whole thing hasn't been easy for me as it was, you know?"

"No, I know it wasn't and still isn't easy for you, and I don't mean to make it worse." Then Emily shrugged. "It doesn't really matter now, not if she's passing away soon. … I was hoping there could be some healing done. But, if her death will be imminent, there won't be any reconciliation." Emily slowly stood, rubbing the small of her back.

"One other thing." Ainsley stood too. "You put her to bed last night, right?"

"Yes. Why?"

"I wondered if anybody came in afterward?"

"Not that I know of, but I certainly can't say for sure. I went to bed right after that. Why?"

Ainsley shrugged and didn't say anything.

"Why? Was the room left in an odd way or something?"

Emily persisted, looking around. "Looks fine to me."

"Yeah, it's fine. I just … I wondered. It's nothing."

Emily looked at her for a long moment. "Now is a good time to tell me if something is wrong."

"I'm sure it's my imagination."

Emily nodded. "I'll go make a cup of tea and lie down. Roasted veggies are in the oven, but I could use a rest. I don't know whether Kascius is coming back tonight or not. I think he is, but, before I deal with all that energy and anger, I could use a little break." She slowly waddled out of the room.

Ainsley stared at her as she left. Then Ainsley turned to Bella on her bed, picked up the medication bottles, and carefully hid them. Ainsley didn't know if it was her imagination or not, but it sure seemed that some of the medication had gone down faster than it should have. And, if it wasn't Ainsley's doings, and it wasn't Emily's, that meant somebody else had been here. Somebody who had a reason for Bella to die a little faster than she needed to.

That thought unnerved her completely. Not only did she have Kascius back here again but always hovering in the background was Angus. Although he made a great potential villain in this mess, it didn't mean he had anything to do with it. And, then again, if it wasn't him, who was it?

Ainsley picked up her cold tea and headed to the kitchen, surprised to find Kascius here, as if he were waiting for her.

"WHAT'S THE MATTER?" he asked.

"I'm not sure," Ainsley replied.

"Mam got upset, looking for her medicine."

She nodded. "I put it away."

He stared at her. "Why? Or maybe that's normal. I guess I need to know where it is, in case I have to give it to her."

"Do you know how much to give her?" she asked, eyeing him shrewdly.

"No, I haven't a clue. Isn't it written on the bottle?"

"Sometimes yes, sometimes no," she said in a cryptic tone. Then she heard Bella calling out for her. Ainsley quickly grabbed a glass and filled it with water, before leaving the kitchen.

He watched her, as Ainsley walked quickly into Bella's bedroom. Ainsley produced the pill bottle, and then walked over to the side of the bed. "Here you go, Bella. It's all right," she said in a soothing voice. "I'm here now."

Almost immediately his mother calmed down. "Oh dear, thank you, dear. My medicine is gone. It's all gone." Then her voice dropped to a whisper. "I think that man took it."

"What man?" Ainsley asked. But Bella's gaze darted furtively to Kascius, who stood in the doorway.

"I didn't take her medicine."

At that, Ainsley nodded. "She gets this way every once in a while. No need for a fuss."

"That's a little disconcerting." Then he watched Ainsley measure the dose and, with a glass of water, held it to Mam's lips. "What is that medicine for?"

"She's on a cocktail for her heart, anxiety, and a couple other things," she murmured. "Don't in any way think this is anything other than end stage. She's not quite ill enough to die from any of her conditions. She's a diabetic. She has congestive heart failure. She's heading into renal failure, with dementia as well. Time hasn't been easy on her."

He stared down at this woman he barely knew. "Is there anything I can do to help?"

She looked at him and then nodded. "Can you get us some more water, please?"

With that, he grabbed the two glasses and headed back to the kitchen. He brought back water in a clean one this time.

After delivering the water and checking his mother again, he was amazed at how much she was soothed by Ainsley's presence. Then he headed back to the kitchen, where he grabbed a to-go cup and quickly refilled it with coffee from the pot.

The last thing he wanted to do was to stay here. It was early morning, but if he could do something on his War Dog case, he would do it. First off, he wanted to go check out the address that Badger had given him, which may or may not be related to any of the addresses the police had.

Kascius sent off a text to the cop he had contact with, asking for an address so he could take a look, scouting from the outside. Since it was nearing seven o'clock, Kascius figured maybe somebody was actually on duty. When his phone rang, as he stood in the kitchen, he realized who it was and smiled. Quickly he answered. "Good morning. Kascius here. Does this mean I get an address?"

"No," the detective said, already exasperated. "You need to stay out of this. I told you that."

"Driving around to check out what's going on in a particular area isn't getting my nose into anything." He reminded himself to stay the course and to be calm. "My concern is for the health of Beamer, the War Dog."

The cop hesitated. "I'm not here to argue with you."

"And I'm not here to cause trouble, though that may not

be how it appears. I'm stuck here, sitting on my hands and wishing I could be doing something productive. I'm not that good at waiting."

At that, the cop sighed. "That's always the worst, isn't it?"

"It sure as hell is. Plus, I have people I report to as well."

At that, the cop snorted. "That's never fun. Okay, I'll give you the address, but I'm telling you. If you contact anyone, there will be hell to pay. Drive by but don't stop. Got it?"

"I won't, but it will give me an idea of the layout and the neighborhood. It will give me a lot of intel, in case we do need to move quickly."

"It wouldn't be a case of *we*," the cop snapped.

"Right. In case *you* need to move quickly." Kascius rolled his eyes. "I'm not here to cause you any trouble."

"Yeah, but somehow I get the feeling that your idea of not causing any trouble will cause me trouble."

Kascius laughed at that. "I sure as hell hope not because I do think our goals are pretty well aligned here."

"What's your goal?" the cop asked sharply.

"Primarily, find the War Dog and get Beamer away safely. However, as a human being, I am also obliged to help in shutting down the rest of that dogfighting ring."

"My goal includes getting convictions, plus shutting them down and rescuing the rest of the dogs. We need to make sure that we get all these bastards."

"Oh, I agree with all that too. The question is whether we can make it happen or if already too many eyes and ears are at work, which will make it harder than it needs to be."

"Are you saying you think somebody is talking? And you better not be saying somebody is talking in my world."

"I'm thinking about a couple things. That kid at the airport wasn't working alone and probably had somebody to pass Beamer off to. You said that address was empty, with no sign of the War Dog. So someone warned him beforehand. The kid? Or someone else? I'm also wondering if the father who adopted Beamer had this planned all along."

"That would be really miserable if he did," the cop said thoughtfully.

"I've never quite understood why they went to all the time and expense of bringing a dog all this way that they supposedly didn't have a chance to bond with yet. They get out of paying for the flight, since supposedly Beamer was lost by the airport employees at the destination airport. Nobody will let me see the video footage, so I don't know if that's true or not." He struggled to keep his voice calm.

At that, the cop laughed. "God, from the sounds of it, we've really done you wrong."

"Not at all," he said, with a big grin. "But you know what it's like to sit and wait, knowing full well you could have had it dealt with already."

"Sure, but even though we have common goals, our actual end results aren't aligned when it comes to this."

"Maybe not," he said instantly, "but no way we're on opposite sides of this."

"No, but methodology is important. Plus, you're not in America now."

The cop's tone had turned snide. "Actually I'm half Scottish on my dad's side and half American on my mother's side. Born and bred right here."

At that came a note of surprise. "Oh?"

"Yeah, so I get what you're saying. I do, but it doesn't change how I feel about this. I don't give a damn what government it is. That War Dog..." Kascius stopped to check his anger, knowing it would do more harm than good at the moment. "Beamer deserves a better life than he's been handed so far. And, when he gets put into that ring, he'll die."

"Damn, you're nothing if not persistent," the cop suggested. "Go check out that address. I'll come and meet you there if I get a chance, but I've got a meeting first thing this morning."

"I'll hold off for an hour if you want. Then I can meet you there."

At that, the cop laughed. "Make it two hours, and that works. In case you haven't noticed, most of us aren't even out of bed yet."

"That's because you're such a sorry lot over here." Kascius laughed at the other man's splutter as he hung up, but the smile remained on his face. He turned with the to-go cup in his hand and pondered his choices. At that moment, he looked over to see Ainsley leaning against the kitchen doorway. He looked up and frowned. She frowned right back. "So, what's the verdict?"

"I'm not sure. I guess it depends on what your agenda is."

At that, he froze and stared at her. "What are you talking about?"

She hesitated and looked at him carefully. "Did you come here for any other reason besides that dog?"

"Aiming to mend fences with my brother Liam, maybe," he said, frowning at her. "I certainly didn't come here to cause trouble."

"Yet trouble always seems to find you." She gave a hard sigh.

"Sometimes, but it's not intentional."

She frowned, then looked back at his mother's room.

"How's Mam doing?"

She shrugged. "I'll call the doctor in when his office opens."

"Problems?" He walked closer and frowned. "Should I be staying here today?"

"If you're asking if she'll die today, I can't tell you that," she offered. "I've already explained that it could happen at any time, or it might not happen for a quite a while."

"Right, and then there's the fact that she doesn't know me."

"That's quite true. She does know Angus, and she's been asking for him this morning."

"Of course," he murmured in a neutral tone. She looked at him sharply, and he shrugged. "He's always been her favorite."

At that, she nodded. "I got that from looking after her for the last while."

"How has Angus been with her?"

"Generally he asks me to leave the room, so he can spend quality time with her. And I'm always more than happy to do so."

"Why is that?" he asked, studying her features carefully. "Is something here I'm not understanding?"

"I don't know, but I'm a little concerned about something, and it happens to coincide with your arrival."

Pouring her a cup of coffee, he walked over, motioning at the kitchen table. "Maybe you should sit down and explain that comment."

She shook her head. "No, I won't. Not yet. It's not fair to the family who hired me."

He stared at her in astonishment. "I'm not the bad guy here. If there's a problem that I can help with, I'm more than happy to do whatever you need."

"The question is whether you've done something to help a little more than what most people would expect," she said cryptically.

He stared at her for a long moment, not liking the implication in her tone. "You know, at one point in time you knew exactly who I was, and there would never have been any hint of something untoward going on. You would have told me what you were worried about. What is going on that would cause you to put something so cryptic out there?"

She flushed, then shrugged. "I've never been in this situation before, and it's making me very uncomfortable."

"And you don't want to elaborate?"

"No, I don't. I want to speak to the doctor first."

"Fine. But, whenever you get ready to fill in the family—and that includes me, regardless of how some people might see me—I'll be there. For now, I'll go off and do what I can with my job." And, with that, he headed for the front door. Just as he was stepping out the door, he heard her call out.

"Wait."

He hesitated, stared at the front door for a moment, then slowly turned, but he could sense that same frustration and anger inside him. "What?" he asked, his tone harsher than normal.

"Are you coming back today?"

"Of course I'm coming back. I've been staying here, and I told Liam that I would get a hotel room, if that was something they wanted me to do. So far, he wants me here. Are you telling me that I shouldn't stay?"

"No, I'm not telling you that at all. But I can tell you that she isn't particularly happy to see you."

"Of course not. Yet everyone said she was looking forward to seeing me. Presumably she doesn't recognize me, and she doesn't want me in there," he said, trying hard to hold back the bitterness.

Ainsley frowned at that. "I didn't realize Bella felt that way. Until I saw her this morning. Until then she was smiling whenever we talked about you. But almost in a vacant way, as if you're not real."

"I'm not Angus, you mean. I've never been Angus, and that's a fact of life," he said, with a wave of his hand. "Now, if you don't mind, we've raked up enough family drama today, so I would just as soon go back to avoiding or missing out on it again." And, with that, he turned and headed for his truck.

He might be early for the meeting, but he'd be damned if he'd stay there and listened to any more veiled accusations. He didn't have a clue what Ainsley was talking about, but one thing he knew for sure was that there wasn't anything nice about it.

CHAPTER 4

AINSLEY STOOD IN the kitchen, staring down at the cup of coffee Kascius had put in her hand, biting her bottom lip. She should have said something different to him. Anything different. Instead she'd gone down the worst pathway possible and had basically accused him of something, yet hadn't come right out and said it. She had gone blank.

The thought that she should have said something cut like a knife, and she flinched. Said what though? She was still standing here when Emily stumbled into the kitchen after her recent nap.

"Rough night?" Ainsley asked her friend.

"Crazy dreams," Emily muttered, as she headed for the coffeepot. "The closer it gets, the more scared I am." She gently rubbed her tummy.

"Yet, there is no reason to be alarmed, is there?"

"No. I don't know. I just can't help but worry." She looked over at Ainsley. "How is Mam?"

"She's okay, but I have a call in to the doctor."

At that, Emily sobered. "Right, are you thinking it's time?"

"No, not necessarily. Why does everyone keep asking me that? I want her medications checked to ensure she's doing okay. Maybe run some lab tests."

"Is it worth it when she's obviously coming to the end?"

"She is. I don't know what that end means," she replied gently.

Not exactly sure she knew what that meant either, Emily shrugged and sat down gently on the chair. "Good Lord. I'll be so happy when this baby is here," she whispered.

"I'm sure you will," Ainsley chuckled. "It's a pretty exciting stage of life for you."

"Especially after waiting for a very long time," she said, groaning. "I can't believe it'll finally happen."

"You're past the worrisome stage, I think. At the moment you aren't in any danger. Even if the baby was born now, chances are he'd make it."

"Technically, in terms of weeks, yes, that is true, but that doesn't mean anything in terms of the baby's health or guarantee that everything will be fine. I don't know what could cause an early birth," Emily said, "but believe me. All these things are enough to keep me awake at night."

Ainsley nodded sympathetically. "Let's keep your thoughts positive. You don't have too much longer to go, so happy thoughts," she said cheerfully.

"No, it's not too much longer, but the days seem as if they are getting longer and longer."

She laughed at that. "I hear you." When her phone rang a few minutes later, she excused herself from Emily, "I'll take this call. It's the doctor." She headed back in and checked on Bella, as she answered the phone.

"I got your message. What's the matter?" the doctor asked.

Hesitating, she said, "I'm not sure."

Surprised and a little confused, he said, "Why don't you explain, and we can go from there?"

She hesitated and then suggested, "I'm wondering if it would be better to move her into hospice."

"That is something the family specifically didn't want to happen. Come on. What's bothering you?"

She looked at the doorway and hesitated. Walking over, she closed the door and then quickly explained about the medication.

"Do you think somebody is giving her extra? Maybe it's someone who isn't capable of looking after her because they're a little too stressed and a little too busy," he asked shrewdly.

"It could be. I don't know." Just mentioning this bothered her a lot.

"Do you want to stay there longer?"

"What do you mean?" she asked.

"Be a live-in nurse." Bluntly he asked, "Are you afraid for your patient's life?"

"I don't know," she snapped right back. "It seems foolish for anyone to do anything. She hasn't got much longer."

"Look. I'll come by and confirm she's doing okay and that we don't need to adjust the medication, which is possible under the circumstances. Maybe we can manage the symptoms you're seeing. Personally I think she is right where she needs to be. It's also where the family wants her."

"I know," she agreed, feeling foolish for even bringing it up, but, if she didn't, who would?

"Has anything changed in the family? Is there reason to suspect that somebody would be trying to kill her?" he asked.

"There have been some changes. As you know, Emily and Liam are due soon with their first baby, and Kascius, the eldest brother, is back for his first visit in a very long time."

"Which would also be suspicious timing," the doc noted

thoughtfully.

"Yet, it almost feels too suspicious, since he's only just arrived."

"Right, that would make me a little nervous too. Anyway I'll come by in a bit. Give me an hour or so."

And, with that, Ainsley had to be happy. She double-checked on Bella, pulling the covers up around her and checking to ensure the room was warm enough. Then she walked back out to the kitchen. "The doctor will swing by in an hour or so."

Emily nodded. "We'll do whatever is needed," Emily murmured. "We've looked after her this long. I'm sure whatever is required at this point in time will just be one more stage of the process. Who knew the process of dying would be so difficult? I don't think it always is," Emily added, "but it's not as if I've had tons of experience with it. Do you get terribly attached to your other patients? To the point that it's painful to leave them?"

"I think everybody gets attached to a certain extent," Ainsley confirmed, looking over at Emily. "A lot of my cases have been unclear as to what the outcome would be, but, in a case such as this, that's not an issue. It's clearly end-of-life. But I don't want that end to be painful. Bella has been doing pretty well so far."

"She has, hasn't she?" Emily agreed, with a smile. "She was always very sharp, very intelligent." She smiled, and the affection was evident in her voice.

"That's interesting." Ainsley looked at her in surprise. "I never really saw that aspect of her."

"No, of course not." Emily laughed. "She did a good job of playing almost a game with it, so nobody ever really understood what she knew and what she didn't know."

"Interesting," Ainsley murmured.

But Emily smiled and laughed. "She was pretty cagey. She used to play her husband quite a bit too. I watched the games from a distance, wondering what she was up to. Sometimes she would tell me, and sometimes she wouldn't. But she always knew that I was on to her, so we had a very different relationship than a lot of others. I understand she had a lot of ill will toward Kascius. … I'm surprised he didn't say anything to you about it." Emily eyed Ainsley curiously. "You guys were close at one time."

"That was a long time ago," she said firmly. "Plus, it was a mess at the time because of my own brother."

"That's right. You lost him somewhere around that time, didn't you?"

"Yes." She nodded. "But time does help heal a lot of old wounds."

"I'm glad for your sake." At the same moment, Emily yawned. "You know, I feel as if I worked all night, and now, even after a nap, I'm already exhausted."

"Go back to bed," Ainsley urged. "You don't have to be up right now."

"Don't I? I need to be here when the doctor comes."

Immediately Ainsley shook her head. "I don't think so. He's doing a regular checkup, humoring me as much as anything." She could sense Emily staring at her intently, as if looking for the truth of it.

Finally Emily nodded. "If you don't mind then," she replied, stumbling to her feet. "Good Lord, I'm feeling pretty wasted." She looked around and asked, "What about Liam? Have you seen him?"

"Liam has gone out to the fields, as far as I know."

"And Kascius?" she asked, looking around.

"He was here earlier, but left, ... something to do with the job he came for. I don't know any more than that."

"I'm such a terrible host." Emily yawned again. "Almost anything appears to be too much right now." She patted her belly. "I'm so desperate to make this pregnancy come off without a hitch."

"That's what you need to focus on." Ainsley smiled. "Nothing else matters."

"Thank you for that. You've been a really good friend."

"Hey, we all just want to see this baby do well. Go get some rest. Nothing else is important right now."

She watched as Emily stumbled off to her room. She turned back toward the kitchen, wondering what she was doing here and whether she was making too much of it all, when Angus walked in the front door. She stared at him, hating how her gut clenched when she saw him.

"Hey," he said cheerfully. "How is everything here?"

"It's all good. The doctor is on his way to check up on Bella."

He winced at that. "God, that's terrible." He shook his head. "Too bad I'm here."

"You can always leave again."

He rolled his eyes at her. "You'd like that, wouldn't you?"

She deliberately chose not to say anything more to antagonize him. All the time he was very hostile and edgy, so the last thing she wanted was to get into an argument with him.

When he walked over to the coffeepot, he picked it up, frowning. "Of course the coffee is all gone." There was disgust in his voice, but she didn't say anything to him. He was a big boy, and he could put on another pot if he wanted to. The fact that he never seemed to make it that far always blew her away.

"I'll be in your mother's room. Better I wait for the doctor with her."

He looked back at her, with a scrutinizing gaze. "Is there a problem?"

"Nope. Not that I know of," she replied cheerfully, then picked up a glass to take some water in to Bella while she was at it. As she walked in, she noted a bit of residue on the glass. She frowned as she looked at it and realized it was the glass that she had handed to Kascius to get more water.

She'd seen a bit of something on the bottom of the glass earlier but hadn't really thought about it. And now, with the glass clutched in her hand, she wondered if this was seriously a problem. How could she get the doctor to worry enough about testing it?

The stray thought weighed on her. Was she being foolish? It seemed so in some ways, but, at the same time, she couldn't let it go. A mistake at this juncture could mean shortening a life, ... Bella's life.

As she looked down at her patient, she had to wonder if Bella would even want to be kept alive longer. What if somebody was trying to make her days easier? Tormented by all the possibilities, Ainsley sat in silence.

When the doctor arrived, she tried hard to take a slow and steady pace to the front door, but it seemed as if she were almost running. As she glanced around, she saw Angus watching her from the living room.

"What's the rush?" he asked.

"I was trying not to wake Emily."

He shrugged. "It will be good when that damn baby pops out."

"Why?"

"Everybody is always catering to her," he said in disgust. "What's up with that? Women have been giving birth since time began."

She stared at him but had already reached the door, so she opened it to let the doctor in.

He smiled at her, as she held a finger to her lips. She wanted to make sure that Angus couldn't see or hear anything more, and she led the doctor through to Bella's room, trying to talk to him naturally. Inside the bedroom, she closed the door gently, then turned to find him looking at her.

"Seriously?" the doctor asked.

She shrugged. "I don't know what it is, and I totally get that I'm probably coming off as a hysterical caregiver. But I don't know what else to say." She walked over, then picked up the glass she had retrieved. "This is the glass that was in here this morning. When I asked Kascius to go get me some water, he left it in the kitchen and brought in a clean glass."

"But you can't be sure because you didn't see it in the kitchen."

"No, I did, and I saw it here first. It's one of the reasons I sent him for fresh water. The glass was pretty dirty looking, but I don't know what made it that way. I had a chance to see it again not long afterward, and there is definitely a powdery residue at the bottom." She produced the glass for the doc to see.

He stared at the glass, frowning. "I wouldn't be so upset about it."

"But it's obvious that she's sleeping more and is less alert than before by far."

"Which, given the passage of time, is very normal," he

noted, speaking gently. "You know very well that the drugs tend to do that."

"I do. I know all that. Believe me. It took a lot for me to call you with this."

"Let me take a look at her, and then we'll talk some more."

She stepped back to give him some room. When he was done, he frowned at her. "She's definitely failing, but I'm not sure it's anything more than what we would have expected at this stage."

"I know, and that's a problem."

"She's not very lucid, and I don't know that somebody would have given her more medication in order to make her less so. It doesn't sound as if she's there much anyway."

"Sorry. It goes back to that whole thing about me being overly cautious."

"Not at all. I've certainly seen more than my fair share of the ugly side of humanity, but what we do need to do is not oversimplify things. So, I'll take the next step, and hopefully we can get to the truth. I can get the substance from the glass analyzed. Then at least we'll know that much." He took it from her and added, "I suppose you want me to keep it between us for now."

She walked over to the en suite bathroom counter, picked up an empty bag for the glass, and handed it to him. "Yes, please."

KASCIUS SAT IN his rental vehicle across from the address. It was a residential street, lined with houses on both sides, but a bit more rural, with adjacent fields full of lots of fences, cross-fences, and even electric fences. It was the use of electric fences that cinched it for him. The fact that anybody would use electric fences pissed him off. In most cases, animals could be trusted to have that experience once and never again, but, in a case where there was probably dogfighting, Kascius wasn't so sure.

He got out and walked up and down the street, trying not to make it look obvious, but a stranger and a strange vehicle would do just that, letting the neighborhood know something was going on. He didn't want to tip off anybody inside the suspect property but figured it was already too late for that.

Still, he hopped back into the truck and drove down several blocks and came back around. When he did, he found the cop sitting at the far end. He hopped out and walked to the police vehicle. At that, Detective Sinclair rolled down his window. "What did you see out here?"

"Lots of cross pastures, lots of electric fences. I have the names being run down by my department, as to who and what can be there, but that's not happening very fast, and there is little to nothing on the owners so far."

"Yeah, well, … welcome to Scotland. I deal with that every day." He shook his head, as he stared over at the property. "I don't know anything about this place, but I can't see anything that looks particularly suspicious."

"Then you're not looking for the things that I'm looking for. This is a perfect spot, particularly in the back, to have training and possibly dogfights too."

"How do you figure that?"

Kascius quickly explained the details of this location that he had pulled from an aerial photo.

Sinclair frowned. "Do you really think the War Dog is

here?"

"I do, and, more than that, I think that they probably know that we're looking for him."

"That's not good. We shouldn't even be sitting here then."

"Yet a lot of other neighbors are around here too."

As they talked, Kascius watched an older lady get into a vehicle from a house across the street and drive away. He looked over at the cop. "I'll go see if I can talk to her."

He asked, "Why?"

"Because she's a neighbor, and chances are she knows more than a lot of people."

At that, the cop nodded. "Okay, let me know what you find out."

"You don't want to come with me?" he asked, with a note of humor in his voice.

"No, it's probably better if I don't at this point. If you find something, then it will be a different story. But you know how people can be about talking to the police. I'm sure you have run up against it too."

"I sure have," he said, with a sigh. "I'm on it."

With that, he hopped back into his truck and slowly followed the older lady down the street until she turned into a grocery store parking lot. Quickly parking, he hopped out, walked over, giving her plenty of time to see him coming. Introducing himself, he told her that he was looking for a dog and that there had been some talk of a dog at her neighbor's property and wondered if she knew anything about that.

She looked at him. "They always have dogs over there. A lot of dogs."

After he asked her a few more questions, she held up a

hand. "I think that's a bit more of interrogation than I can handle. Why are you asking about this?"

"Curiosity, plus I'm looking for a specific dog."

"I really don't want to rat on my neighbor." She frowned at him. "Yet always something is going on over there. I do hear quite a bit of partying and maybe fights going on. The place is buzzing at odd times." She shrugged. "Outside of that, they are huge sports fans," she said, with a reminiscent smile. "My husband was like that. The minute the game came on, he was jumping all over the furniture and generally making a fool of himself."

"Is that what you think is happening over there?"

"I have no clue." She shrugged. "What I can tell you is, they stick to themselves, and I've never had a problem with any of them. Honestly, I think if I needed help, they'd probably come running."

He nodded and smiled. "That's the kind of neighbors to have."

"It is." She gave a nod. "It's hard to find that these days. The world is changing."

He quickly asked several other questions, but she didn't appear to know anything. He wondered if she could really be that unobservant or if she was on their side. Suspicious, he thanked her and walked away, but he kept an eye on her.

When he was out of her sight line, he positioned himself so he could see her. She hadn't gone too many steps toward the store before she had pulled out her phone and had made a call. He smiled at that. If he had ever needed confirmation of what his gut was telling him, he got it with that one call.

When she came around a corner to see him leaning against a wall, she immediately stopped and froze.

He nodded. "So, when your friends are convicted of a

crime, and, as it all comes before a judge and jury, that phone call you just made will make you look guilty as well. So now you're an accessory."

She almost seemed to wilt in front of him. "I didn't do anything. Believe me. I didn't."

"Maybe not, but you warned them, and that is something the judge will not take kindly to."

"No, no, no," she cried out. "I didn't do anything."

"Yeah, you did. Who did you call?"

She stared at him in a panic, putting her phone behind her back almost instinctively, such a two-year-old child's reaction.

He raised an eyebrow. "The cops will love that."

"Cops?" she asked, the color draining from her face.

"Did you really think this wasn't a police matter?" Kascius asked her.

"You said it was an American War Dog."

"Your friends are into dogfighting, and that's where the War Dog has been taken to. But that's okay, you get to keep your little antic to yourself for now—until it becomes public knowledge, when the details of this all come to light later on. I've already texted your name and address to the detective investigating the matter."

"No, you don't understand," she cried out in panic. "I can't be caught up in that. My family would never forgive me."

"Yet apparently you didn't think about that when you tipped off these guys. So why on earth would you have done that if you are such a lovely law-abiding citizen who cares so much about the health and well-being of dogs? Which obviously you aren't and you don't. So, what's the deal? Are you gambling on the dogfights or something?"

She shook her head. "No, you don't understand."

"No, I sure don't, and, until you explain it, I won't understand."

"But I can't," she said fretfully. "If my daughter finds out, she'll be so ashamed."

"Yeah, I wonder why?" he snapped, not letting up. "Do you think your age will save you? It won't. I can tell you that right now."

She stared at him and held her hand to her chest, as if she couldn't breathe anymore.

He shook his head, pulled out his phone, and called the detective. "She's definitely involved. She's not exactly telling me why or what her involvement is, but she called someone and gave them a heads-up."

He heard the detective swearing on the other end.

"You've got a lead at least," Kascius pointed out.

"What is that?" the detective asked.

"Her phone. She's got the phone number for the dogfighting group. If you want to meet me, she's right here beside me." He gave him the name of the shopping center they were standing nearby and said, "What I don't know is what they'll do when they find out that she's been caught. Are these guys willing to kill for their involvement, or do they consider this a sideline?"

"Oh, I think they're pretty committed. I'm on my way to you."

"Good enough. I'll stand here with her and make sure she doesn't get shot in the meantime," he said in disgust. And that's what he did. As soon as he hung up the phone, he crossed his arms and stared at her. "Still think your neighbors will help you now that the cops are involved?"

She looked beyond upset but remained silent.

Kascius wasn't having anything to do with it. He'd seen an awful lot of people in his life who used all kinds of ruses, and he wasn't about to be taken in by somebody who used her age to get away with this crap. He waited until the detective pulled into the parking lot.

When she realized it really was the police, she started to panic. "No, no, no, I can't."

"You should've thought about that before you warned your neighbors." Kascius glanced at her. "We don't have a whole lot of patience with criminals, particularly ones involved in illegal gambling and God only knows what else, particularly when they hurt the dogs to do it."

"I don't know anything about that," she said immediately.

"Yeah, well, I don't believe you. I highly doubt that the detective will believe you either."

At that, the detective strode toward them, took one look at her, and his eyebrows shot up. "Seriously?" He looked over at Kascius.

"Yeah, seriously. She phoned and let them know that I was out asking questions and looking for the War Dog. She's been stalling ever since, saying she doesn't dare get caught and that nobody is allowed to tell her daughter, who will be so ashamed of her."

Sinclair turned to her and frowned. "It sure would be nice if she had thought about that before she got involved with these criminals. No doubt that your neighborhood will be abuzz with the news pretty soon," he told her, motioning toward his cruiser. "So let's get you down to the station."

"No, no, no," she cried out. "I can't."

"Why not?" he asked, looking at her doubtfully.

"Somebody has to be there to feed my cat," she replied.

Kascius groaned. "Yeah, so you care about the cat, but you don't care about the dogs? Got it. I'll go take care of your damn cat," Kascius muttered in a disgusted tone. "But you go with the detective." He turned to Sinclair. "As long as she gives me permission to go in, I'll feed the cat and put out fresh water."

He nodded. "Do that. And call me when you're there."

"Will do." Ignoring the neighbor lady's continuing diatribe, he headed toward his vehicle.

Suddenly he felt an odd sensation in the back of his head, and, as he turned, he looked over at the neighbor lady, and shouted, "Duck!"

The shot rang out hard and clear.

CHAPTER 5

LONG AFTER THE doctor left, Ainsley sat at Bella's bedside. She wondered and puzzled through why anybody would want to hurt Bella at this point in time. Unless it was for compassionate reasons, and maybe then Ainsley would understand. But considering how close Bella was to dying, it didn't make a whole lot of sense. Not all that long ago, Bella had still been capable of jotting things down, talking lucidly, and watching TV, but she had slipped quite a bit in recent weeks and was into a quicker decline now. Was it a natural slip in her health or had somebody helped her along?

Once the suspicions started, it was really hard for Ainsley to stop them. The trouble was, she had almost accused Kascius of being involved earlier today, and now she could see that he probably had nothing to do with it, but his arrival was a hell of a convenience, if someone had done something. The timing made it all seem even dodgier.

Three other people were in this house with full access to Bella and her meds all the time, but others came and went as well, though it was more likely to be one of the three. That bothered her terribly because she had been friends with Emily and Liam for a very long time and didn't want to even consider that they could be involved. But because she didn't want to absolve them immediately, she had to carefully consider that option. Then there was Angus, the easy scapegoat.

But to think that he had gone through with this was even more terrifying. He was scary, and he bothered her a lot, but she never would have thought he would do something to seriously hurt his own mother. He loved her, so what possible motive could there be? Although, according to Emily, Angus would get money or some part of the farm, which was something that had Liam on the hot seat. Yet what good would it do to make that whole timeline go faster? She didn't understand any of it.

She waited until Bella woke up again and stared at her. Bella was a little disoriented. "Good morning," Ainsley greeted her, "although it's well past noon now. How are you doing?"

Bella looked at her and plucked away at her bedcovers. "I'm fine," she whispered. "Can I have a cup of tea?"

"Yes, you absolutely can." She helped Bella to the bathroom, then came back and refilled her water, while the teakettle boiled the water for tea. As soon as it was ready, she brought her a hot cup. "How are you feeling?"

Bella smiled. "I'm feeling better today. The world is not quite so foggy."

"Good. Makes for a good day."

At that, Bella nodded and asked in a hopeful tone, "Is Angus here?"

"No, I don't think so. He was here this morning, but he left. You were sound asleep at the time, so I didn't wake you."

At that, Bella frowned. "I always want to see Angus. You know that," she grumbled.

"I get that, but you also needed to sleep."

But Bella wasn't to be appeased. "I want to see him when he comes back." Then she snapped, "No, I want to see him now."

"Okay, I can contact him, but he mentioned he had some places to go."

"Of course." She immediately nodded and sat up a little taller. "He's a very important man, you know."

"Of course he is," Ainsley replied, not sure what Bella was getting at or why she thought Angus was important. "Kascius is here too, although he's not in the house at the moment."

She looked at her, confusion clouding her gaze. "Kascius?"

At that, Ainsley studied Bella curiously. "Yes, your eldest son. He's home for a visit with you and your other two sons."

"I have only two sons."

By the time the day was done, Ainsley had spent as much time with Bella as possible. She had been in a better mood for most of the time, although she'd had several more naps. When Ainsley had a chance, she asked Bella if she wanted her journals.

Bella looked at her. "Maybe," she murmured. "Just leave them close by."

With that, Ainsley pulled them out of the drawer and brought Bella a pen to use. Before the end of her day, Ainsley checked to see how Bella was doing, but she was half-sleeping, half-awake, in an altered state—which Ainsley had seen before, with people not very far from death. Ainsley hesitated, unsure if she should leave.

Bella even seemed to notice Ainsley squirming and smiled at her. "I'm not dying anytime soon. Go ahead and leave."

She looked at Bella in surprise, as this was one of the most lucid comments Bella had made in a very long time.

Bella shrugged. "I want to see my son again."

At that, Ainsley frowned. "Okay." Still, she hesitated.

Bella looked at her sharply. "Angus."

At that, Ainsley nodded. "I did send him a message saying that you wanted to see him."

"He's a good boy. He'll come when he can come." She smiled. "He's always been a good boy to me."

Ainsley nodded, not sure what she was supposed to say to that. Bella had three sons, and, after seeing how differently the three were treated, she couldn't imagine the life Kascius had growing up. Nobody but Liam and Emily seemed to even want to see Kascius. All this time Ainsley had been blaming Kascius for not showing up to see his mother, but Bella wasn't even willing to consider him as her son.

Yet everyone had told Kascius that Bella was looking forward to seeing him, which seemed totally wrong. Had Bella said something to Liam and Emily that Ainsley wasn't privy to? Because, what Ainsley heard consistently, whether Bella was having a good day or a bad one, was that Angus was Bella's favored child. Even with today evolving to be a good day for Bella relatively, she still wasn't showing any love for her eldest son.

Ainsley tried one more time. "You know Kascius is here."

"I don't want to see Kascius," Bella snapped. "That boy is nothing to me."

"Interesting," she murmured. "I didn't realize you didn't want to see him."

Bella looked at her sharply. "Why would I? He was

nothing but trouble. It was easier when he was a long way away."

Ainsley winced at that. "Most people would say that old troubles shouldn't matter when you're close to the end of your life."

"Trouble that just creates more trouble," Bella argued, with a defiance that Ainsley hadn't seen before. "I don't want to see him."

"Okay, so do you want me to tell him to stay away?" she asked, since she wasn't in that position to make that decision for her.

"Yes, absolutely, but he won't come anyway."

"Come where?"

"He is over there in the Americas," she snapped, with a biting tone. "He can stay over there. It's easier to be polite."

"You don't love him?" Ainsley asked, trying to quell the horror in her heart.

"No, I never have. He was a terrible baby, and then he broke my husband's heart. How could I want anything to do with him?"

"And that's it? Just one mistake and it can't be forgiven, even now?" Ainsley asked.

"There will be no forgiveness."

Ainsley felt sick, wondering if she'd ever known this woman. And fumbling right after that was Ainsley's own heart, as she thought about what Kascius had been through with his family, and then her part in sending him away. "And what about Liam?"

Bella waved her hand at that. "Liam is an opportunist. Neither of those two are my special boy," she stated, with a beaming smile. "Angus is the only one who counts."

Ainsley stared at her in shock.

But Bella was already pulling her diary toward her and starting to mutter to herself.

Ainsley didn't even know what to say. She slowly walked out and saw Emily sitting at the kitchen table, having a cup of tea, lost in her own thoughts.

Emily took one look and hopped up, and asked, "Are you okay?" Her tone was concerned.

Ainsley's breath gushed out, as she motioned for Emily to sit back down. "She had some really mean things to say about Kascius that I didn't really understand were a part of their relationship before."

"Oh, yeah." Emily winced, as she retook her seat. "Unfortunately Kascius has always been the one who got hit with it all."

"Why? What did he do?"

"It's all because he didn't want to be a farmer."

Ainsley stared at her for a long moment. "But she didn't have anything nice to say about Liam either. I guess you know that as well."

"I know," Emily acknowledged. "I don't think Liam understands it though. He has always tried hard to be the responsible one and to be here and to take care of everything here at home, here at the farm, everywhere. Bella has never really seemed to care about anybody but Angus." Emily glanced around and added in a whisper, "And you always have to watch to make sure Angus isn't lurking around somewhere, listening from the shadows."

Almost at the same time they heard the sound of the front door opening, and Emily immediately widened her gaze and pinched her mouth shut.

With that, Ainsley got the message loud and clear.

As Angus stepped into the kitchen, he groaned. "Ainsley,

what does Mam want now? That old bat is driving me nuts."

"That old bat loves you. In fact, you may be the only one she loves."

At that, he shrugged, topped off with a smirk. "Of course she does. I'm her favorite. I always have been." And he walked into Bella's bedroom to the sound of instant cries of joy.

"Are you okay?" Emily asked Ainsley in a low tone.

She nodded. "I will be. I don't know what I'm supposed to do about this scenario."

"There's nothing you can do," Emily said simply. "None of us found a way all these years, so I doubt Mam will change now."

"This is something I haven't really seen before. Anytime there's a death in a family, you get to know all the dirty secrets, but this is over the top. I truly feel sorry for Kascius. He didn't deserve to be kicked out of the family, way back when, just because he didn't want to be a farmer."

"And they gave two-thirds of the farm to Liam, and the last one-third Bella keeps until her death. Though, at the time, Liam didn't really realize what was happening. He does now," Emily stated. "Still, it was hardly fair."

"And Angus?"

"For Angus, it has brought up all kinds of hard feelings, and he has been holding a grudge for a very long time. He wants the whole farm to sell it. Which isn't what his father wanted, and it breaks Liam's heart."

"And Kascius?" Ainsley asked.

"Actually I think Kascius had made his peace with whatever was going on in his world all those years ago. I think he is probably the only one who did. Once Angus found out, it only made him more obnoxious," she muttered. "As for

Liam, he went to work. That's what he does. He doesn't really know any other way to handle this but to keep working and to keep doing the best he can with what he's got."

"You know what, Emily? That's good advice. Maybe that's the best way to handle this. Just keep on working and hope that everything works out for the best."

"I don't know that it's worked out that well, since we still have all this drama, but it definitely has served to keep Liam busy and moving in a positive direction." Emily patted her tummy and added, "We'll make do one way or another, and I'm sure we'll be fine."

"You will," Ainsley offered, with a supportive smile. "Especially now that you're getting the one thing you always wanted. That baby will go a long way to making you happy."

"I'm happy regardless." Emily laughed. "As long as Liam loves me, and this child comes through healthy and safe, everything in my world will be fine."

At that, Ainsley got up. "I'll head on home. I'm exhausted."

"It was an early morning."

"Yeah, it was at that."

Emily cocked her head and gave Ainsley a long look. "Is everything okay with the medication? Do we need to change anything?"

"No, and she's already had most of everything for today anyway. She gets one more dose tonight, and that's it." Hesitating, she looked back at Emily. "Just keep an eye on it, will you?"

"Sure." Emily eyed Ainsley curiously, as she used the table to get up. "Is there a reason? Is there something specific to keep my eye on?"

Ainsley shrugged. "I don't know, yet something feels off to me."

At that, Emily sat down hard. "In what way?"

Ainsley was sorry she brought it up. She shook her head and smiled. "It's just me being me. You take care of yourself, and don't worry about it."

"No," Emily said immediately. "I can't help but care, so I do need to know what you're thinking. Especially since I've been feeling that things have been a little off myself, and I haven't been able to put my finger on it."

At that, she stared at her friend. "Do you understand what you're saying?"

"No, because I don't know what it is that's off, but it sure seems something is not quite right."

Ainsley hesitated, then shrugged. "Maybe we'll both feel better in the morning."

"I hope so," Emily replied. "I can't really focus or worry about anything other than the baby right now." She patted her tummy. "That's occupying every moment of my time."

"That's a good thing." Ainsley turned to leave.

Emily asked, "Ainsley, do you still hate Kascius?"

She shook her head at her friend. "I've never hated Kascius." She looked toward Bella's room, confirming the door was closed. She placed her finger against her lips and whispered, "Honestly, I never have. I'm not sure where anybody got that idea."

At that, Emily pointed toward Bella's room. She wasn't sure if that meant Bella or Angus but wouldn't put it past either one of them. She sighed. "Not that it matters anyway. That time is long gone."

"Maybe so, but that doesn't mean there isn't time to begin anew." Emily sighed. "I have no idea why I blurted that out. I'll go lay down for a few minutes." She got up and waddled her way back to her bedroom, leaving Ainsley all alone with her thoughts.

As she walked out the front door and headed to her car, Ainsley wasn't exactly sure what was going on in that house, but it no longer was the warm, loving family home she'd always been so jealous of. She wasn't sure what the difference was. The only thing she could put a finger on was the fact that Kascius was home. The reunion with his family was something she had wondered about for a very long time, but it wasn't exactly the happy homecoming she had imagined.

KASCIUS WAS MORE than frustrated after a day of being kept on the sidelines, even though he had hustled up a valuable lead for the authorities. He found something for the cops to go on, yet here they were, back at the police station, taking too much time sifting through it all. He'd been pushed off to the side, even though he had been promised some things, which were then taken away. The shitty thing was that he ended up spending the bulk of the afternoon sitting at the police station, waiting, hoping that somebody would let him in on the details of the investigation.

The most he got out of one frustrated cop who needed more coffee was that the neighbor lady was talking now, after being shot at. Thankfully for her sake, they'd missed, but it had the desired effect of making her much more amiable to the police. She'd even given Kascius the keys to her house so he could feed her cat.

Kascius nodded. Probably was by one of the dogfighting ring. Not that Sinclair would tell Kascius anything.

He texted Badger several times, wondering if there was anything his boss could do. Finally Badger replied. They had gone above and beyond their usual effort, and it still wasn't looking good. At that, Kascius had gotten up and walked out, realizing he was wasting his time here. The cops could get as mad at him as they wanted, but he was after a War Dog that needed help, and Kascius sure as hell wouldn't let Beamer disappear or be killed, which was constantly on his mind. And he was chomping to get into the game. This was BS, and he was done with it. Political friendships be damned. Beamer was too important.

Kascius made another pass by the neighbor lady's house, letting himself in to feed and water her damn cat, while familiarizing himself with the layout, so he could navigate the area in both daylight and dark conditions. He wanted to see what was going on in that property. With his second pass just now, there wasn't anything more to find, outside of a lot of electric fences. He didn't see a whole lot in the way of security, but, with that many dogs in there, particularly fighting dogs, they didn't need much of a security system anyway. Free and out of the cages, the dogs could raise one hell of an alarm. However, they'd only be let out of their cages at fighting time, and that would be it. With nothing else left to be done, Kascius headed back to the family farm.

As he drove up the driveway toward the house, a car came toward him. Immediately he recognized Ainsley. He also noted that she was upset, being all too familiar with that look on her face. He pulled off to the side and stopped, waiting for her to stop and to talk with him, but she drove right past him, with a speed that concerned him even more. He immediately turned the truck around and followed her.

She drove straight to her house, and, when she got out,

she turned on him and glared. "Why are you following me?"

"Why are you upset? Is Mam okay?"

Getting to the point was his style, so her surprise then settled back slightly. "Bella is fine."

He could see that Ainsley had tried to wipe the tears off her face, but they were still drying on her cheeks. He gently brushed her cheek. "What happened?"

She shook her head. "It doesn't matter."

"It matters to me. Did she say something to upset you?"

At that, she shook her head. "Your family is a hot mess."

He stopped and stared, then gave a clipped nod. "That's possible, but I haven't had much of anything to do with most of them for a long time. I've kept in contact with Liam and spoken to him many times. When I've called, I've always spent a moment or two speaking to Mam, though that never seemed to go that well most of the time."

"I'm surprised it went well at any time," she snapped. Then she took a deep breath and surprised him with her next words. "I didn't realize they hated you so much."

He stared at her calmly. "I don't *think* Liam hates me. Unless you know something I don't."

But she was already shaking her head. "No, I'm not talking about Liam. It's your mother—and Angus maybe."

"Oh, yeah, the same old BS." Kascius stared off in the distance over her head. He could see her sister in the window of the house. "That's old news. Might as well leave it at that. I don't think it'll go anywhere, and it's not likely to get resolved anytime soon."

"She'll die hating you. You know that, right?"

Her clogged voice and suggested tears were on his behalf? "I don't think *hate* is even the right word, unless I'm mistaken. It seems too strong, as words go. Mam cut me out of her life when I didn't become what they wanted me to become."

"Your father too?"

"Yeah, he led the pack on that one. It made me never want to have kids or to settle here because there is that constant reminder of what a shitty son I was."

She shook her head at that. "But it's not for them to judge you that way. That is on your shitty parents, not a reflection on you as a son."

He gave her a wry smile. "It's funny to hear that now from you. I don't think you would have said that all those years ago."

"I was an idiot," she said bluntly. "I was overwrought and didn't know what I was saying." He stared at her in shock. She shrugged. "Yeah, that's been a long time coming, but I did wake up eventually. I was pretty devastated over my brother's death and all the work that I'd put into trying to keep him alive. When my attempts didn't work, I felt like such a failure." She raised both hands. "God, I don't even know why I'm telling you this."

"It helps me to understand what happened between us back then," he answered, staring at her in wonder. "But how could you even think you were a failure with your brother? You were everything to him."

"Yet he died."

Again he heard a bitterness he wasn't expecting. "He was very ill," Kascius pointed out. "You did everything humanly possible to help him."

She took a deep breath. "Look. This is something I've never told anybody." Then she hesitated, and he waited, knowing that some truths were hard to get out. "I think he committed suicide."

He stared at her, a sick feeling in his stomach. "I can't imagine why he would have done that."

"He was so very sick."

"Ah." He thought about it for a moment and nodded. "If it was his end stage, and he didn't want to fight any longer, maybe he did. I don't know what that feels like, and I certainly can't judge him for it. I can't even begin to comprehend such a nightmare. But, even if he did commit suicide, is it a deal breaker in how you view your brother now?"

She stared at him and sagged against her car. "No, I can't hold it against him," she whispered, "but there's always that horrible feeling that I did something wrong. That he needed something from me that I didn't have to give, I guess."

Kascius shook his head. "That's guilt talking right there, and you're afraid you could have done more. It's normal that we're afraid, that we wonder if we didn't do enough when someone dies. In this case, I can't imagine that it's true. You gave him all you had. I know you did."

She stared at him, and he shrugged, then continued. "I get that, for the longest time, people didn't see me in a great light. No one understood it, and that's another reason that living here was difficult for me, but I do have some insights into human nature. Mostly because I had such a crappy childhood, I think."

At that, her eyes widened. "Wait. You mean they treated you that way when you were little too?"

He smiled. "Liam went out with my dad on the tractor, starting when Liam was a little guy. He absolutely loved it, but I hated it. I hated the noise, hated being out there in the middle of nowhere. Maybe I would have grown up and accepted it over time, but I never got that time. Right now, the thought of a tractor doesn't thrill me, but being out there in the fields does. I would be quite happy with the peaceful existence that comes with this lifestyle now. Back then, it was my doom."

"Are you saying you're okay with what your parents did?"

"It's Liam's farm. That was really never, ever in doubt. It was his—and Angus's of course."

"I didn't even know that Angus had a stake in the place."

Kascius nodded. "Apparently. It's not so much his stake as much as it is my mother's. They've already looked after her for all these years, so I think everyone is resigned to the fact that Angus will be around, being a pain in the ass for the next twenty or thirty years. Whereas, from my point of view, all of the farm should go to Liam for looking after Mam." He shrugged. "Yet I have no say in it."

She hesitated again. "So, what is it you're not telling me?"

"Nothing. By the way, thank you for sharing your concern about your brother. I loved your brother, and he was one of my best friends. But I sure as hell can't stand in judgment if he did decide to terminate his life a little early. If it saved him one day of pain, agony, and torture, then I don't feel bad about it. But if you think he did it out of depression or his inability to handle whatever life was dishing out, find it in your heart not to judge him or yourself. You did what you could. Make peace with that and move on. The last thing he would want is you feeling bad about it all these years later."

She sniffled and brushed her eyes. "I've told myself exactly that so many times since he died, and, although I get it intellectually, it's still very hard emotionally."

He immediately nodded. "Of course it is. Nothing's easy about any of this. When you love somebody you've spent a long time with, even though you're mentally prepared in some ways, you're not emotionally prepared because how could anyone ever really be prepared to lose someone they love?" he said quietly. "It's hard and rightly so, and nobody can help you through that process, although it might have been easier if you'd had somebody to be there for you."

She snorted at that. "You mean, like you, the man I sent away, so I would never, ever have to go through another experience like that again?"

"Maybe." He studied her, wondering at the changes time had wrought in her. He wasn't the only one to grow up apparently. "You never wanted to nurse anybody or to deal with anybody who was less than whole."

She stared at him. "That's what you thought I meant?"

He looked at her, one eyebrow raised. "Was there any other way to take it?"

"I guess I can see how you could have come to that conclusion," she muttered, wrapping her arms around her chest. She shook her head. "But it wasn't that. In fact, it wasn't that I didn't want to have anybody in my life or to have anybody broken in my life. I hated what the military had done to my brother, and I hated the fact that you were bound and determined to go not only back into military service but to transfer to the US. The fact that you even had the ability to do that blew me away."

He shrugged. "My uncle was in the military over there, if you remember."

She nodded. "Right, and that kind of makes sense. So, he sponsored you or some such thing, right?"

"Yeah, there was a point in time when there was a transfer window open, and some of us could make the trip across, and they were looking for young men. That's how my cousin Karl went over as well."

"Sure, they always need more young men to go die for their country. And yet, here we were, dying without you."

"Yet that's not quite true," he said calmly, crossing his arms as he studied her, wondering at how belated this conversation was, many years too late. Yet it had nothing to do with finding Beamer. "You might not like the fact that I wasn't here. However, if things had changed, I probably would have stayed."

"But then again, you would have still been in the military here and ended up like my brother."

He frowned. "Is that what the problem was? I wasn't even thinking of going into the US military, except my uncle offered me the opportunity to go see a whole new world. Plus I wanted to get away. And that offered me the opportunity to do so. After we blew up, I accepted it. I needed a change of scenery."

She nodded. "I get that now, but, back then, I had no idea that your family life was as rough as it was."

He shrugged irritably. "Don't make it out to be more than it is. I had enough of a problem dealing with the family back then, and I sure as hell don't want to rehash it now."

"Would you have come back after her death?"

"Maybe. Not to see her get buried but more to see my brothers and to see if there was anything I could do to help them."

"So, you do care about Liam?"

"I always have," he stated calmly, "and I would like to think that he knows it."

"I think Emily does. I'm not so sure about Liam. I don't even know if he really understands how much is going on right under his nose."

"Do any of us?" he asked her curiously.

"No, maybe not."

"You still haven't told me what had you so upset that you were crying as you drove home just now."

She hesitated. She obviously wasn't done with the conversation they'd been working on, and neither was he. "I can't talk about it. It doesn't really help me."

"What part doesn't help you?" he asked, trying to keep his voice calm. He hadn't really expected all this conversation to happen. But then he had tracked her down, so what had he expected?

"I was looking for clarity, I guess," she murmured. "With your mother dying, I guess I was expecting more emotion on your part. I have to admit, over the last few months, she has gone downhill, I've judged you for not coming home. And even when you did, it seemed you've been more concerned about whatever this crazy assignment is, versus spending time with your mother. I didn't really understand, until I talked to Bella today and realized just how much she holds against you."

He nodded. "Yeah, it's always fun to have your family open up like that. There are a few things that a person would rather not have open for public consumption."

She winced. "I'm sorry. I thought, when she was asking to see her son, that maybe it was you, and she was confused. I was trying to convince her to hear you out and to clear the air, hoping I could then call you, and maybe you would come and visit," she whispered in shame.

He nodded. "But instead of a potential happy reconciliation, you probably got an earful about how she doesn't give a crap about me."

"Kind of, yes." She smiled softly. "It sure helped me understand more about who you were."

"Who I was, or who I am?" he asked, with a laugh.

"In a way, I guess they're both the same, aren't they?"

"To a certain extent," he murmured. "What difference does any of that make now?"

"I didn't get it back when we were going out. I had no idea how much of a mess your family was for you."

"How so?"

"Your father had just died."

"A year earlier but, yes, and he had just given Liam the farm officially. And, even though I knew what was coming, it wasn't exactly the same thing as knowing that it really had happened."

She nodded. "Your father wasn't a nice man, was he?"

"No, he sure wasn't. His farm was everything to him, and, if you didn't agree to get on board with that, then you were nothing to him, as I found out rather quickly."

"That's a terrible way to raise a family."

"But don't forget how that part had really happened earlier. My father died ten years ago, and I had managed to stick around, working locally in the military with your brother, until he was injured, then died."

"Right, that's when I went to pieces."

"Maybe, but I think it was more of what you were looking for in terms of your future that split us up, if that's where this is going."

She looked at him and gave a half smile, shaking her head. "I don't know how I forgot that you're such a straight shooter, but you are right about that."

"I find that speaking directly is easier than innuendos and half-spoken truths. We broke up because you didn't want anything to do with anybody else who was broken," he declared, with a shrug. "And I was going back into the military because that's where my heart and soul were, with the potential of ending up in a condition that was unacceptable to you. Heading over to the US was just another way for me to get a little farther away from the heartache that was here. That doesn't change anything, and it's water under the bridge at this point."

She hesitated, then shrugged. "I guess I wanted to say that I'm sorry."

"What are you sorry for?" he asked in genuine confusion. "You spent a lot of years nursing your brother. You did a great job at that, and I really appreciate the fact that you did it because he was my friend. I know that he was a bit stressed and confused at the end, but that can't in any way negate what a great person he was."

She smiled. "There was a bit of an investigation after his death, but it was quickly closed down."

"What investigation?"

"The doctor did wonder if he had gotten access to his medications."

At that, Kascius shrugged. "And, if he did, then what?"

"I don't know. I guess the question is whether anybody helped him do it," she said, searching his face.

"I didn't." Then he frowned. "Have you been thinking that all this time? That I might have …" He stopped and stared. "That I might have killed your brother or helped him kill himself?"

She shook her head. "No, no, that never occurred to me. The generic thought occurred to me when the doctor brought it up as to whether anybody else could have given my brother his medication, but it's not as if he were immobile. If he'd wanted to make that superhuman effort, he could have gotten up and got his medication on his own, and he was certainly lucid enough to have taken it himself."

"Okay, Ainsley"—Kascius stared at her—"where is this going?"

She stared back in the direction of Bella's house. Then she opened her mouth, and suddenly it came out in a rush. "It's occurred to me that somebody might be giving your mother more medicine than she needs."

He stared at her in disbelief.

"What? Now hang on a minute," he said in a very low tone, as he studied her carefully. Surely she hadn't meant that the way it sounded. "When you say that, are you saying that she's not taking it herself, but that someone is potentially trying to kill her?"

CHAPTER 6

THE NEXT MORNING, Ainsley woke and stared around at her bedroom, groaning. She'd had a horrible night. Memories of trying to calm down a very upset Kascius had dominated. He finally calmed but with that coldness cloaking him that was even scarier. He'd promised to not say anything but would keep a close eye on what was happening.

She'd explained that the doctor was involved and would get the glass tested, but it could very well be that there was nothing suspicious and that it was just her nerves. He nodded at that and didn't say anything more. He'd left very quickly afterward, not looking for any further explanations, almost as if he'd decided that he would sort this out himself, and that scared the crap out of her. The last thing she wanted to do was go back to that house today. But her job was to look after Bella, though Ainsley hadn't expected the job to turn in this direction. She still couldn't get over the fact that she and Kascius were talking like normal human beings. It had also been a shock to realize she hadn't gotten over him. He tugged at her heart in ways no one else could.

She'd known, but knowing it and acknowledging it was a whole different story.

Her sister was in the kitchen when Ainsley finally got out of the shower and dragged herself down for a cup of coffee.

"That was quite the heart-to-heart you had last night." Sibel looked at her sister curiously, over the rim of her mug.

"It was."

"Couldn't have been good though because you looked upset and then went straight to bed."

Ainsley looked over at her sister and nodded. "Yes, it was very difficult."

At that, Sibel shook her head. "You know that relationships are supposed to make you feel better, not worse."

"Until you realize how badly you messed up. I had no idea his home life was so awful."

Sibel looked at her. "What's that got to do with your relationship with Kascius?"

"It's not about the relationship," she stated, not wanting to go into all the details. "But yesterday at their house it was a pretty ugly affair, as Bella flat-out told me that she really wants nothing to do with him."

At that, Sibel looked at her, one eyebrow raised. "That seems harsh, especially under the circumstances. What does a person have to do to deserve that?"

"I'm not sure he did anything," she clarified. "According to Emily, the minute he didn't want to be a farmer, his parents wrote him off. And even that was predisposed in a way when he was very young, simply because he didn't enjoy riding around on tractors with his dad."

Her sister stared at her.

Ainsley continued. "Honestly, it was upsetting coming from Bella, but one has to consider her situation. But then more details came from Emily, and I've known her for a long time. She is not a person who makes accusations, and she would never make up something like that or embellish the details."

"No, she wouldn't. Frankly their father always scared the crap out of me," Sibel murmured. "There was something very unrelenting about him. He'd look at you, as if you were absolutely nothing, as if your very existence was a bother, regardless of what you were trying to do. You were in his way, and you better move fast to get out of it."

There wasn't a whole lot Ainsley could say to that, but she agreed. "And then of course we talked about Lanson."

Her sister's gaze was sharp, as she stared at her. "What about our brother?"

"Just how his death affected me and how I didn't … want anything to do with that full-time caregiver lifestyle anymore, plus how it really affected me that he went back into the military, and I knew Kascius wouldn't stop, even though it was obvious that he could end up like Lanson."

"He *could* end up like that, but it's not a guarantee by any means." Her sister stared at her curiously. "Besides, our brother loved what he did."

"That made it right, I suppose?" Ainsley's outburst seemed to surprise Sibel. Yet Ainsley felt as if she was always guessing at Sibel's thoughts. Unlike their brother, Lanson, who'd been an open book and who'd loved life, until he'd been injured.

"I'm not getting into an argument about the benefits or the lack of them when it comes to going to war," Sibel began, "but I certainly understand the man's need to be protective and to look after his family and to find that warrior within. That's all our brother was trying to do, and he loved his life, up until the death he had. But he didn't blame that on his injuries. He was content and happy as a soldier."

"Yet his injuries were responsible for the way he ended

up," Ainsley argued. "He never did recover, even after he went through multiple surgeries because of the lost leg and the back injuries. He was in terrible shape throughout it all."

"I know that." Sibel cupped her hands around her coffee mug. "And we've never really talked about it, partly because we were always on such opposite ends of the scale. You were so angry that Kascius would leave. That he had the nerve to leave you. Honestly, you were also terribly angry that Lanson was as badly injured as he was. I didn't really realize then that you were blaming him or blaming the military for the way he ended up. That doesn't seem terribly fair to me."

"Nothing's fair about any of this." Ainsley stared at her sister, wondering how she hadn't understood this before. "If we had talked earlier, I might not have been quite so adamant."

"You were grieving, and you already had such a predisposition to this whole thing that I'm not sure anybody could have talked to you at the time."

"Was I really that stubborn?" Ainsley asked. "That closed off?"

"Yeah, you were," Sibel agreed, with a bright smile. "I love you dearly, but you were not easy to be with. And honestly, the fact that our brother died as he did, even though he was really close to recuperating and making it through, I think made it that much harder for you. It seemed we got him through so much, and then, at the end of the day, his body gave out."

"And that's quite possibly how it was." Ainsley stared at the steam coming off her cup. "I'm not sure whether that's the right way to look at it or not, but the fact of the matter is, when it came to the end, we couldn't do anything for him."

Sibel got up, put on toast, then looked back at her sister. "I presume you're leaving to return to Bella soon."

"Not a whole lot of choice at the moment." Ainsley took a sip of her coffee, wishing she could go back to bed.

Her sister nodded. "You need to learn to take things a little less to heart. Keep some perspective, so you can see beyond what you're feeling."

"I wonder though. It feels as if, in many ways, I blamed Kascius for all of it back then."

"I'm sure you did. Honestly, if you guys hadn't been such a hot number at the time, I would have been all over him myself. I stayed away because I didn't want to be a terrible sister, but, as far as I was concerned, he was one hell of a catch, and I couldn't understand how you let him go."

This morning's conversation was enough of a surprise already, but to hear her sister verbalize her feelings about Kascius was an even bigger shock. "Seriously?"

"Absolutely. That man has always been a hot stud, but he never gave me a second look. It was always you."

There was no bitterness in her tone, for which Ainsley was grateful. "You don't blame me for that, do you?"

"For chasing him away?" she asked, with a wry smile. "I did for a while. But you were just as unhappy as he probably was when he left, so not a whole lot to blame you for. Besides, I've moved on." Sibel flashed a cheeky grin. "Speaking of which, Henley is picking me up after work, and I probably won't be home for the weekend."

"Weekend?" she asked, and then she blinked. "Good Lord, it's Friday?"

At that, her sister laughed. "It is. Please take this the right way, but it might be time for you to get a life."

"It seems to be past time for me to do that," she agreed.

"Maybe, when this is all over, I can."

At that, her sister nodded and smiled. "I'm really glad to hear that. Kascius is a good man. I don't know anything about his childhood or the mess that he had growing up, but, if it impacted his life in any way, he made the best of it, and he didn't hold it against them. Or you, for that matter."

With that, her sister snagged up her things. "I'm running late, so talk to you later." Taking a bite out of the toast, Sibel headed out the front door.

Not exactly the conversation Ainsley wanted to be left with. She got ready for work, and, by the time she arrived at the house, Emily was curled up on the couch, dozing. "Hey, Emily," she murmured, gently trying not to wake her friend if she was in a deep sleep.

Emily opened her eyes, yawned, and said, "So glad you're here."

"How is Mam?"

"She had an uneasy night. She kept crying out for her husband."

"That's not unusual." Ainsley nodded in understanding. "Particularly at the end."

"Maybe not, but it was still a little distressing."

"How is Kascius?"

"He's fine," she said, with a bright smile. "Honestly, it's such a blessing to have him here. It's really good for Liam to get to spend time with him."

"Did they always get along so well?"

"Yes, that was the thing about Kascius. He never held Liam responsible for any of the mess in the family. But Liam always blamed himself because he could never find a way to make the family whole again and broker any peaceful existence. It's really bothered him."

"You can't blame him either. Liam is the least confrontational man I know."

At that, Emily chuckled. "Oh, he does have a temper. He just doesn't let it loose that often. More important, he's a really good man. I lucked out."

"Yes, you did." Ainsley chuckled. "It does seem that all the good men are gone."

"Ah, they really aren't though." Emily gave her a gentle smile. "They may not be quite so visible or close to the surface as others, but they're out there." She got up, then stopped and winced, as she grabbed her lower back. "Good Lord. I wanted nothing more than to be pregnant, but right now? I want nothing more than to be done with this pregnancy. Sometimes I am really uncomfortable."

"Go to bed," Ainsley suggested instantly. "Give your body more rest. I'll put on some tea and bring you a cup."

Her friend looked at her gratefully. "You're not here to take care of me. I have to keep reminding myself of that."

"No, you don't." Ainsley laughed. "We're friends. I don't need a paycheck to get my friend a cup of tea." She pointed toward the stairs. "Go. Before you know it, the baby will be here, and you'll be wishing you were back to being pregnant, so you could sleep all day."

Laughing out loud, Emily headed toward the stairs. "I am really happy you're here today. I know I still have a while to go, but it doesn't feel like it."

On that note, worried at her friend's words, Ainsley watched carefully as Emily headed up the stairs. Then Ainsley walked into the kitchen, where she put on the teapot.

She quickly did up the dishes, even though that wasn't part of her job either. But helping a friend was one thing, and a paycheck and needing something to keep her busy was another. It was still pretty early, and she looked up when Kascius darted in through the kitchen door.

He stepped into the kitchen. "Good morning."

"Morning."

"Everything has been fine overnight," he murmured with a nod, almost as a veiled reference.

She stared at him. "That's good. I guess I'm not really expecting anything other than that at the moment."

"Good, I do have to get going. Are you okay?"

"I'm fine. Go." She waved him off. "Honestly, I'm fine."

"Good." Then he hesitated. "I could have quite a busy day, but call me if you need anything."

"We'll be fine here. You go do you," she said instantly.

He smiled. "You always were good at handling these things."

"I'm not sure what 'these things' mean," she noted, using her fingers for air quotes, "but I've never been one to shirk away from whatever needed to be done."

"Exactly." He walked toward the front door, tossing back, "I'll grab something to eat in town."

"If you had gotten up a little earlier, you could have had breakfast."

"I did get up early. I spent some time with Liam."

She watched as he walked out the door, feeling a terrible sense of dejection as he left. She couldn't help but walk over to the front window and watch as Kascius hopped into his vehicle and drove away. She was so damn sad that, even after all this time, she was supersensitive to his every word, to his every movement. Almost hypervigilant of his very presence.

It wasn't something she would want him to know. From his actions, she had no way of gaining any insight into whether he still cared or not. She also knew that she'd walked away from any right to have a say in his life. Still, it hurt to see the casual nature of his gaze.

She wasn't even sure why he'd followed her back to her house yesterday. It wasn't something she could even explain when her sister had asked. At first, Ainsley had taken it as a good sign of sincere concern, but then, once they had talked about her brother and all his questions were suddenly centered around his family, she realized it didn't have as much to do with her and had everything to do with his family. A scenario that was just messed up, even now creeping her out.

With a heavy sigh, she made the tea and walked up to Emily's bedroom. She knocked gently, and, when she heard her friend call out, Ainsley entered. "Here you go. Just stay tucked in bed and relax."

Her friend smiled. "Thank you. How is Bella?"

"I haven't been in yet. I'm heading there now with her tea."

She closed the door on Emily, then returned to the kitchen and picked up the second cup of tea and walked in to talk to Bella. As soon as she entered, she froze with a sense of dread, one she had never experienced before. Bella lay on her back, her mouth open and her face contorted. As she raced to the older woman's bedside, Ainsley put down the tea, so she didn't spill it on her. "Bella, Bella?"

But there was absolutely no doubt. Whatever had been wrong was well past anybody doing anything to help her with it now. Ainsley checked for a pulse, but it was too late.

Bella was already gone.

A BLACK TRUCK sat back from the properties the cops were getting ready to search. Kascius was grateful to be given some contents of the reports that the detective had shared. "I really do appreciate this."

The detective shook his head. "Turns out you have some friends in high places. We still can't have you go to any of these raids in real time. But, in the spirit of cooperation," he said in a mock tone of respect, "we're supposed to allow you access to our reports, so we can try to provide support in the recovery of the War Dog. I sure hope you guys look after your people as well as you look after these dogs."

Kascius smiled at that. "I'm not at all sure that we do. Yet you've got to start somewhere."

At that, the detective looked at him, startled, then nodded slowly. "That's not a bad way to look at it. And I've got a soft spot for dogs, so I'm totally okay with it. I'm still pissed to have a dogfighting ring operating right here in our midst. We've known there was one but couldn't catch a break to find it. We've been after it for a long time."

"I'm glad to know that—regardless of what happens—this mess has resulted in a raid on the place."

"Exactly, but remember?" He shot him a look. "You don't get a weapon, and you don't get to go in, not until it's all clear."

"Got it." He shifted his stance and studied his surroundings. They were parked several blocks away, as they waited for everybody to get into position. Kascius really missed having a weapon, but, hey, he hadn't routinely carried a weapon in a few years anyway, and he had enough skills to do without one. Even though he might be on the slower side now, he was confident he could still hold his own. He looked over at the detective. "Just tell me that I get to go in and look for the War Dog."

"We'll all be going in, looking for the dogs. We've also got dog trainers and even a vet on call, if we need them."

"I don't even know what to think about that. Obviously, if we find the animals there, then we'll call your local trainers and the vet. However, if we call them, it also means the animals must be injured and need them."

"Regardless I presume they must be checked over, and then we'll have to find interim foster locations for them, so we'll need the vet and others involved. Transporting and housing fighting dogs has to be handled carefully."

Kascius wouldn't argue with that. He hoped that the War Dog he sought would be found and would be okay. He turned his phone off, and everybody stood around, waiting. Finally they got the go-ahead.

"Okay, we can go in," said Scott, the person in charge.

Kascius had been chomping at the bit to get going.

"Sorry." Scott turned to face Kascius. "I guess I stopped your ability to get in this case earlier."

Kascius shrugged. What could he say? He'd fought hard to get in on this but had met bureaucracy at every turn.

"It's all right now," Scott added. "The warrant has been served, and the lead team is inside right now, securing the scene. Sounds as if not much is there, but come on."

The two cops stepped up and entered through the front door. As Kascius hung back and looked around, the house was unexpected. It wasn't a farmhouse, more a modified villa. He wasn't even sure what the architecture was supposed to represent.

"Are you sure any dogs are in this place?" Kascius asked Scott.

"I'm not sure of anything," Scott declared, staring

around him, "but you're right. This appears to be more of a drug lab than a dogfighting ring."

"Unless they're doing both, or maybe they're using drugs on the dogs."

"That would really suck. But even what we're seeing here should be enough to put whoever is behind this part of it away for a good long time. At least you understand how this works."

"I haven't worked in law enforcement per se, but I did a lot of investigation work in the navy." At that, Scott raised his eyebrows. Kascius shrugged. "Now, I'm footloose and fancy-free, trying to figure out what I want to do with my life."

"Hey, join law enforcement," Scott suggested. "We always need people, especially those with special skill sets, such as yours."

"I'm not sure anyone would consider my talents as skills." His gaze roamed the room. "However, it's not a bad idea."

"Hey, you want to talk to my boss about it? Believe me. I can probably get you an in. We're rather desperate for good men. You are Scottish, right?"

"I am." With a smile he stepped forward and pointed something out to Scott. "Did you see this?" A bunch of photos were on the wall, all of dogs held on large chains, looking more than dangerous.

"These assholes really are working in the dogfighting business, aren't they?"

"Looks like it." As they stepped a little farther into the house, they were greeted by another detective.

"We've got two men, sitting in the kitchen, with pretty smug attitudes. We'll take them in and see if we can get anything out of them."

"If they've got those attitudes, chances are they think you won't find anything," Kascius noted, thinking out loud. Then he looked at Scott sharply. "Do you have access to satellite imagery?"

"We can get satellite. Why?" the detective asked, looking at him.

"Is anybody checking to see if they moved the dogs last night or even earlier this morning? After the neighbor lady called and tipped off these saps? Just to ensure nothing incriminating was on the premises? The neighbor lady called them yesterday morning. They've had plenty of time to move the dogs. We need everybody checking local neighborhoods to see where they moved the dogs."

"Not yet," Scott said, "but I can get our tech team on it right now."

The other detective looked over at Kascius and asked him, "Who the hell are you?"

Kascius shrugged. "I'm part of a friendly division, as I'm after one of the dogs here."

"Right, you're the guy after the War Dog," he said, as if mentally fitting him into some place in his mind.

"Let me know if you see him. Can't believe these assholes are doing this."

"It's a mess everywhere, as it is. The last thing we need is this shit around here. But gamblers will always be gamblers."

"And sometimes I wonder if some degree of gambling should be legalized," Kascius suggested. "Although that quickly becomes too tame for most of them anyway."

"It doesn't need to be."

Hearing a dog barking in the distance, the three men looked at each other and raced out to the backyard.

There they found six dogs in pens, barking madly at the raid team. Kascius eyed them carefully. "None of these are the one I'm looking for, but it doesn't mean they aren't what you guys are after." Looking around, Kascius pointed at the neighbor's property. "I don't suppose your warrant extends over there, does it?"

The detective at his side shook his head. "No, this property only. Why that one?"

"Look at the tracks. A lot of them run in that direction."

The detective started swearing. "Good eye."

"I'm taller than you, so I have a better angle," Kascius muttered. "Actually, from this angle, you could *almost* say it's evidence in plain sight, requiring due diligence to protect the animals."

"Yeah, well, *almost* doesn't cut it, if the whole case gets thrown out," the detective replied.

"How much trouble will I get into if I head over there and take a closer look?" Kascius asked.

The detective looked at him with one eyebrow raised and shrugged.

Casting a last look at the detective, Kascius grinned and bolted over to the property. He didn't even hear a shout behind him, as if they were more or less washing their hands of the strange Scottish-American breaking all the rules. He had no intention of breaking the rules, but, as he bolted over the fence and ducked down on the other side, his phone vibrated.

He checked his texts and found one from the detective, saying, "Be careful, and don't do anything to compromise our case."

Kascius understood that in theory, but he also was here to get and to protect a War Dog. On the other hand, he couldn't be here to save just one, not if there would be hundreds that needed rescuing. He shifted and slid, working his way a little farther in the background among some bushes, and finally ducked low along the fence line and came up around the pastures.

He checked all over the acreage and found what appeared to be about five acres fenced in. A shed was at the back and a big barn. He quickly moved off the fence and behind the buildings. He didn't know whether it was privately-owned land or belonged to the Crown land, but it was definitely open pasture. He sent off a quick text to Badger to see if he could tell him more about the proper owner of this land.

Kascius wandered along that fence line, checking out the back shed. It was empty and appeared old. He kept going across the fields along the back. He focused on the heavy tracks, both human footprints and dogs, following them across the property and over to another property on the other side. Kascius sent off a second text to Badger, asking about this second additional property.

Of course, it was better to take the animals as far away from the target property listed on the warrant, but to have the dogs going to another location they could so easily be tracked to didn't make that much sense.

Kascius came up to a clump of trees and stood silently, then sent a text back alerting the detective of his location and what he was up to. Just then he heard a series of barks. He followed them through the trees, trying to stay upwind of the dogs, so they wouldn't get a whiff of him being here.

As he took a panoramic look around, he quickly pulled out his phone and started taking photos and videos. Then he quickly sent Scott several short clips with a text message.

Seems the dogs are over here. Not sure of the lay of the land yet or who is here, but I've found over forty dogs.

By the looks of it, most of them were separated into pens or crates, in groups of four or five. One big male off to the side was clearly being segregated, yet he howled and growled at all the dogs around him.

Kascius searched the pens, looking for Beamer, but despite all the looking, he saw nothing in the chaotic mix. But then again, Beamer also might be injured enough that he wasn't being kept in this area. Kascius kept moving around the back of the pens, taking a closer look, trying to figure out what he was looking at.

When he got back a text from Badger, Kascius just smiled.

He sent several more short video clips to Scott. When he came around the next corner, he froze and stared because there were the injured dogs he had wondered about. However, what drew his attention was a smaller dog, with a gaping wound on his side, whimpering and looking for assistance.

Kascius swore at that.

Just as he went to stand up, a handgun rested against the back of his neck.

"Freeze."

He slowly straightened, trying to compensate for his leg, as he stepped up and turned to see a man staring at him, with a big grin on his face. "Interesting dogs."

"They sure as hell are, and you're on private property."

"There are no signs," he said immediately, "and this isn't private land anyway."

The guy looked at him. "What the hell do you know about it?"

"What shouldn't I know?" he asked. "I came looking for

property to buy over on the other side. When I rounded the corner, I saw the dogs. Are you breeding them? You really need a vet for that one." Kascius pointed at the one dog with the gaping wound. "That's not healthy. It'll get infected, and the dog needs stitches."

"Don't worry about the injured dog." The gunman gave him a hard glare. "Matter of fact, don't worry about any of these dogs."

"Yeah, so it's your property, is it?"

"It sure as hell is." He spat on the ground, but his gun hand never wavered.

"I don't believe you," Kascius declared, crossing his arms over his chest, glaring right back at him. "I think you're running these dogs on Crown land, though I don't have a clue why."

"None of your business. What the hell are you even doing here?"

"I told you what I'm doing here. The question is, what the hell are you doing here?"

"I'm the one with the gun, so shut the fuck up, bitch."

"I don't give a shit if you got a gun or not, unless you're prepared to put a bullet between my eyes and deal with the consequences of such a thing. So, best be done with it, or you better put that thing away."

"Yeah, or what?"

Kascius instinctively moved fast. He grabbed the gun and pulled it down, so that the shots fired harmlessly into the ground. At the same time, he came up with his knee and hit the guy in the groin, then pivoted and flipped him to the ground, and, with a right hand, took a jab at his jaw that knocked him out. Kascius sat back, snatching up the handgun, and said, "There, you little shithead. That's exactly what I'll do."

At that, he sent another text back to Scott. Taking off his belt, Kascius quickly tied up the prisoner on the ground and checked the gunman's pockets. Then Kascius checked over the dogs again and grinned, as he finally located the War Dog. He was segregated off from the injured ones. At that second-look confirmation, Kascius let out a whistle, commonly used with K9 training, a whistle that a War Dog should recognize.

Kascius watched as the dog lifted one of his ears, and, given the order to come, it slowly limped toward Kascius.

"There you are." As Beamer came toward Kascius, he checked the markings on his phone to make sure and nodded. "Hey, boy. You're Beamer, aren't you? You're a beauty."

At his name, the dog's ears twitched, his head came up, and he looked at Kascius intently.

"Come here, boy. It's okay. You're safe now."

But, in the distance, Kascius heard sounds of people coming. He really hoped it was the cops, but there was no way to know for sure just yet.

He shifted closer to Beamer, until he could get up to the War Dog and quickly slipped a lead onto his collar, so he could take Beamer over to where the injured dog was. Once there, and not sure who was coming, Kascius scooped up the injured dog, which didn't give him any argument. Even with the two dogs, Kascius managed to get them and the unconscious gunman back over to the fence. He got them through the wooden slats; then he dropped his prisoner over first. After that, Kascius climbed over the fence. There, on the other side, he sat down beside the unconscious man and waited.

When the detective reached him, he swore when he took a look at the injured dog in his arms. "Jesus Christ."

Kascius nodded. "Right? Poor thing." With a nod toward the unconscious man, he added, "This is the asshole who pulled the gun on me."

"What gun?"

He lowered the injured dog gently to the ground, then, with a baggie over his hands now, he pulled the weapon from his pocket and handed it over. "This one. Don't mind me. I took it off him because I have this thing about having weapons shoved into my face."

He stretched out his leg, sliding down beside the dog again, and heard an odd sound beside him. He looked up to see the detective staring at his leg. "Yeah, I lost the leg in the last tour, so that has kept me out of the military."

"And you still took him down?" he asked in an odd voice.

"Hell yeah." He looked up, smiled. "And, before you ask, … no, that's not all I can do."

"Damn. You need to talk to my boss about coming to work for us."

"I'm pretty sure they won't let me with this leg."

He nodded. "No, maybe not, but, if you have any interest in working with dogs or coming on as a special constable, I'm sure they'll want you."

"Maybe, maybe not." Yet Kascius eyed him curiously. "Maybe you could put in a good word for me."

"In a heartbeat. We want anybody who can take a weapon off a guy and take him down, especially when unarmed, just as you did."

Clearly breaking open the case and rescuing these dogs had earned Kascius points with Scott.

"Damn, we can use a man like you any way we can get you."

Kascius laughed at that. "Just make sure you get the rest of these assholes."

"We will." At that, his phone rang, and the detective stepped off ever-so-slightly to take the call.

The conversation was hard to keep up with, so Kascius turned his attention to the dogs.

Finally Scott turned around and reported, "Nobody is in the house on the property down at the bottom. This is not a property that we know to be associated with our perp, but, because we've got the dogs and have at least one needing critical veterinary care, we're doing a full seizure, and we've got a vet standing by." He looked over at the injured one and swore. "That breaks my heart."

"Mine too." Kascius hated people sometimes. "Beamer here was staying close to the injured one, and the only reason I was allowed to even get near enough to catch Beamer was because I was looking after the injured one as well. I really want to keep track of both of these dogs."

"Yeah, and do what?" Scott asked. "Are you looking to keep them? I don't even know what the hell the rules are when it comes to this shit here."

"I'll ensure the animals are cared for." Kascius grinned. "We do have somewhat of a prior claim."

At that, the detective rolled his eyes. "I have no idea what the hell that all means at this point, but if you're willing to help look after these guys—"

"My brother has a big farm, so, as soon as these two dogs are good to go, I'll take them back there, at least temporarily."

"Good enough. Where's your brother's farm?"

When he described the location, an odd look crossed the detective's face.

"Why that face? What's the matter?"

He hesitated for a moment. "Listen. We got a call about a death on the property."

"An old woman?"

He nodded.

"That would be my mother then." He stood up, feeling something odd inside him. "We were half expecting it."

Scott looked at him, then took a deep breath. "Maybe you were, maybe you weren't, but her nurse has been arrested for murder."

CHAPTER 7

AINSLEY SAT CURLED up on the single bench, leaning against the depressing graffiti-colored wall in the jail cell, completely frozen inside and out. She had no clue what was going on or why she would even be a suspect. When she heard her name called, she looked up to see Kascius striding toward her. She immediately burst into tears and raced to the bars.

He reached through and wrapped his hands around hers. "I heard, but I don't know anything. What the hell happened?"

"What happened is your damn brother," she snapped. "Angus immediately pointed a finger at me and said that I murdered your mother. I didn't. I swear to God, I didn't."

"Of course not. Did they say anything about why, outside of his accusations, why they would even keep you here? Why they would even suspect you?" he asked, obviously not understanding or having heard the full story.

She took a deep breath. "My brother. I don't even know how they would have known about it."

"Your brother? Why would he even come into this?"

"I don't know, but apparently the cops have had suspicions about my brother's death this whole time."

"Even though it was closed and written off as natural causes?"

She nodded. "But, as I told you, I was worried about it."

"But none of that makes any sense."

At that, a cop came up to him. "Interesting conversation. But part of the reason why we have her here and won't be releasing her anytime soon is because your mother was killed by the same drug that her brother died from."

Kascius turned and stared at the cop. "They weren't on the same medications by order of a doctor?"

The cop shook his head. "I can't give you too many details, but I can tell you that your mother died of foul play."

"How the hell would that have already happened and been investigated so early on?" he asked, staring at him in suspicion. "I get that obviously it's a fresh case, and you have to jump on it, but how is it even possible that you guys found that out already?"

"Because we found medication in her purse."

He reached up, rubbed his face. "Good. So you jumped on something so obvious as that, and she gets fingered for it? Ainsley is a licensed nurse." The cop stared at him, and there was no joy in his look. He didn't like Kascius meddling with their case.

The cop turned back to her. "Do you have a lawyer?"

She shook her head. "No, I don't. Of course not. Why would I? This isn't something I expected."

Kascius nodded. "No, why would you? Let me see who I can roust." He looked down at her, at the empty cell, and asked the cop, "Can she at least get a cup of coffee or something?"

"Hey, this is jail, not a hotel, and this is nothing compared to where she'll end up."

Kascius stared at the cop. "She isn't going to jail. She didn't do this." And, with that, he turned and walked out, leaving her alone.

She stared at the cop. "I really didn't do it. I was just looking after her."

"And helped her on her way, just as you did your brother?"

She felt the tears choking her, pooling up in the back of her eyes. "No. I did no such thing," she cried out.

"Maybe not, but that's not what the evidence is showing."

She sat back down, wondering what the hell had happened. When there was another noise, she looked up to see her sister racing toward her.

"Good God," Sibel cried out. "What are they doing to you?"

"They seem to think I killed Bella. The medication was found in my purse. I didn't even know that they looked in my purse. And who knows why they even thought I would do such a thing." Then her tone darkened. "Except Angus told them I murdered her."

"He didn't mean it, I'm sure. We'll get to the bottom of this, don't you worry."

She shook her head at that. "I don't even know what the bottom of this is," she cried out in frustration. "I even called the doctor to let him know that I didn't like something that was going on."

At that, her sister asked, "You did what?"

Ainsley shrugged. "Yesterday. I was suspicious when a glass left in Bella's room overnight had an odd powdery substance in the bottom."

"Who found the glass?"

"I did, but I didn't give it much thought. I just gave the glass to Kascius to take out to the kitchen and to get me a fresh one with water for Bella. Then I grabbed the suspicious glass afterward, with no idea who had given it to her. I gave it to the doctor and told him that I wasn't sure what was going on. I thought he was sending it off to be analyzed. But why the hell would they suspect me?" She knew that the cop was sitting there listening in, but she didn't care because she wasn't saying anything except the truth.

Her sister stared at her. "Good God. Why didn't you tell me?"

"It was just a suspicion, and I had no way to know what the powder even was, but I won't go telling tales when there wasn't anything to say for real," she said, raising her hands in frustration.

At that, another man walked in. Tall, dressed in a black suit, he looked at her and snapped, "You need to stop talking."

Ainsley frowned at him. "Who are you?"

"I've been retained as your lawyer, and, as of right now, as of this moment, you need to stop talking to anyone, unless I'm right beside you."

She slowly closed her mouth, then looked at her sister and shrugged.

Sibel nodded. "We'll get to the bottom of this." And, with that, she backed away.

The lawyer waited while the cop opened up the cell door. "You're being released on bail."

"Who posted bail?"

He shrugged.

She didn't have a clue what was happening, but, considering she was getting out, she didn't really care at this point in time. In silence, she went through the process of being released. As soon as she got outside, she turned to the lawyer.

"Who retained you, and who posted my bail?"

"I did," Kascius said, from behind her. She turned toward him. He smiled, walked up to her, and pulled her into his arms, holding her close. "You're a lot of things, but you're not a killer."

She felt her tears choking her once again. "Thank you," she whispered, swallowing her sobs. "Not just for posting bail but for believing in me."

"Believing in you is easy. You've always been on the straight and narrow, and I know that."

"And the fact that you contacted the doctor about that substance in the glass is also a good thing," the lawyer noted. "I did hear that part of the conversation, so now we need to go somewhere safe and away from listening ears. I need to know what the hell is going on here. Every single detail. Kascius has brought me up to speed, as he knows it, but honestly, we haven't had a chance to do more than that."

"How did you get that done so quickly?" she asked, looking over at Kascius. "How did you even find him so fast, much less get him here?"

"I called my boss."

She stared at him, finally saying, "Nice boss."

"We have a network around the world." He grinned. "Besides, this is my hometown." He grinned over at the lawyer. "By the way, this is Larry. He and I went to school together."

She stared at Larry. "Thank you."

He shrugged. "Hey, when old friends call, you step up to the plate. I did know you in high school, and I certainly would have agreed with what Kascius said about your character, but I can't take it on faith. We need to talk, and you need to tell me exactly what's going on."

Kascius suggested, "Let's head to a coffee shop or something. We need someplace that's a little private, where she can have some food and calm down."

She looked over at him. "How did you know I needed food?"

"You're shaking, and you've always had low-blood-sugar problems."

She sighed. "And here I thought you walked away and never thought of me again."

"I never stopped thinking about you," he said cheerfully. "But you weren't ready to commit to what I needed you to commit to back then. So, we weren't ready for each other, but that didn't keep us from being friends."

Friends was the last thing that she wanted to be with him right now, but, as a friend, he'd already proven to be a hell of a lot more helpful than she would have expected. By the time they hit a coffee shop, and she was sitting down in a warm space, holding a hot cup of coffee in her hands, she explained the little bit that had happened over the last few days.

"And all of this happened after Kascius arrived?"

"Yes, and, though I didn't bring it up to him, I assumed that he was astute enough to not ignore the fact that he would make a great scapegoat."

"And yet, as scapegoats go, it ended up being you instead."

"Yes"—she shuddered—"but only because of Angus."

"Maybe I'll look like a second-best suspect, or with the suspicions on her, maybe they'll assume that we're in it together," Kascius offered in a wry tone. "I'm not under any illusions here."

She stared at him. "Wow, that was a leap."

"Maybe, but whoever is doing this can't be all that stupid."

She shook her head. "That's why it never made any sense that they were trying to make it look as if you had done it. Since you had only arrived, that would be way too obvious."

"The ability to discern something as 'way too obvious' is a feature of brainpower that some of these criminals often don't have," Larry interrupted. "So, from the top, go over everything, and don't leave anything out."

It took a while, as she tried to remember all the bits and pieces. By the time she was done, Larry had several pages of notes.

He nodded. "The best thing in all of this is that you did give that glass to the doctor and that, somewhere along the line, hopefully, he got it tested."

"I haven't heard from him. Honestly, I wasn't even sure what to do about it. I guess I could have contacted the cops, but I sounded idiotic, prattling on about a mysterious white substance in the bottom of a glass."

Larry nodded. "And, because you were responsible for her, you did the right thing in the sense that you reported it to the doctor. Now, what the doctor did with that, we don't know, but we need to find out."

"You can contact him or I can," she said, pulling out her phone.

"Nope, leave it," Larry said. "I'll contact the cops, and we'll make sure it's all done through official channels. Chain of custody is important, and we need to do things by the book."

She slowly put her phone on the table and nodded. "I don't even know what to think right now." She bit her lip, as she looked over at Kascius. "It would really hurt to think Emily and Liam believe this."

"Right. I haven't talked to them, but I will as soon as I get home. And then of course there's Angus."

"Angus?" Larry asked, still writing down notes.

"My youngest brother," Kascius stated in a hard voice. "The one who pointed the finger at Ainsley."

At that, Larry raised his head and looked at him. "The lazy one."

"Yeah, the lazy one," Kascius confirmed.

She looked over at Larry. "You really do know the family, don't you?"

"Yeah, I do. We were in sports together, and I was part of Kascius's life when his dad more or less kicked him out of the family. So, Liam got the farm." He looked back at him curiously, "I suppose that hasn't changed."

"No, it hasn't changed at all," he agreed. "My mother retained a portion of the farm, and it's expected that it would go to Angus."

"Did she have any rights over the rest of the farm?"

"I'm not sure." Kascius eyed Larry curiously. "Everything went to my mother but the shares to the farm, I thought." Then he frowned, looked at Larry. "Maybe you can clarify that. I don't get anything, but did Angus get more than that? I wasn't privy to the will, as I wasn't in it."

Larry considered that and frowned. "How much money did your mother have?"

"I have no idea. Remember? I got kicked out when I wasn't worthy of being part of the family."

At that, Larry nodded. "Sounds as if you went on and had a better life anyway."

"I did. However, another concern here is that Liam's wife, Emily—you remember her. She was a couple years behind us. She's very pregnant, and she's had multiple miscarriages already. They didn't think that she would make it this far, so the last thing we want is to have her upset."

"Too late," Ainsley whispered. "She was there when I got arrested."

"Ah, crap." Kascius rubbed his temples. "That's something I need to check in on. We may need to get her a nurse." He looked over at Ainsley. "The sooner we get this cloud cleared over your head, the sooner I can get Emily back to being calm too. She'll be absolutely hysterical."

"Have you checked your phone?" Larry asked.

Kascius shook his head and pulled out his phone. "Shit, I'd turned it off because of the police raid I was part of. Then when the detective I was working with told me what happened with Mam, I came straight to the jail to check on Ainsley." He quickly saw he had four messages. He got up and said, "Excuse me. I'll be right back." And, with that, he walked off to the side.

As she watched him go, she faced Larry. "I really didn't do it. Angus immediately accused me of killing his mother. But I didn't. I wouldn't."

"I'm glad to hear that. That's important."

"I can't even begin to imagine."

"As you suggested, Kascius makes a really good victim for a setup here but not necessarily a reasonable one, as in what's his motive?"

"See? That's the thing I don't understand. He wouldn't do this, and it doesn't make any sense at all that he would do this when he'd only just arrived. If he was trying to hide his tracks, he would have made it seem to be somebody else."

"You mean, like you?" he asked seriously.

She stared, her jaw dropping, and then shook her head. "No, he wouldn't do that."

"No, he wouldn't. I wanted to know how you felt about it."

"I'm completely confused at the moment, and I don't understand any of this. If the police had even asked me a few more questions, it wouldn't have been so bad, but Angus just—well, I think Angus probably threw me under the bus right away."

"I suspect what he pointed out was the fact that you had the opportunity, since you were the one looking after his mother, and he also said that Bella was quite upset and included something about her accusing you."

"Oh, *great*. So how am I supposed to argue with a woman's deathbed accusation?" She frowned. "I didn't realize Angus saw her that morning. He wasn't there when I arrived. Or was he?"

"Nothing's ever that simple, but we'll get to the bottom of it eventually."

She sighed and sat back. "I'm glad to hear that," she whispered, a single tear rolling down each cheek, "because I didn't do anything wrong. To Bella ... or my brother."

"Good. Keep that energy, that righteous anger at the forefront. Don't let it ever go, but you also have to be controlled, so you're not the person who keeps giving the police more to go on, even if it's just motivation." Then he looked at her. "I haven't had a chance to talk to Kascius about his return. I presume he came back for you?"

She stared at him, her bottom lip trembling. "I wish he had come back for me, but it was a job that he was asked to do. He is trying to locate a retired American War Dog that was shipped over here and got lost. You'll have to ask him, but now there's something about it getting sold to a dogfighting ring. I honestly don't know very much about it."

"He wouldn't have come back for his mother. No love lost there at all."

"No love lost, but he also wasn't in any negative mindset about it either. She wanted nothing to do with him. He did call Liam to talk to her over the years." She let out a shaky breath. "It makes no sense. What's the motive in killing a dying woman? If Kascius wanted to kill her, he could have done that a long time ago, and it probably would have been much more satisfying. For that matter I have no motivation either."

He smiled at that. "Believe me. Having gone to school with him and keeping in contact afterward, when all that was coming down, I know what he's like and how he was treated by his family. The reality is, the cops will definitely be looking at everybody else, if it wasn't you."

"Good, and so they should. I didn't do it."

Just then Kascius came back over, but the look on his face was anguished.

She bolted to her feet. "Oh my God," she cried out hysterically, when she saw him. "What happened?"

He pinched the bridge of his nose, then took a deep breath. "Emily is in the hospital. She collapsed after you were arrested, and Liam came home and found her on the floor, bleeding. She's in the hospital, and Liam is at her side. But … it's not looking good for her."

Ainsley's hand went to her mouth. "Oh, dear God. Oh God. Can I go there and be with her?" Her gaze shifted between Kascius and the lawyer.

Larry's face was grim when he said, "In any other circumstances, I would say, yes. However, for right now, I'm not sure it's a good idea."

"Why?" She stared at him in horror. Her heart sank, as

she thought about poor Emily.

"According to Angus, she's pretty upset, and she's blaming you," Kascius muttered.

KASCIUS DIDN'T WANT to say that to her, but he had to tell her the truth. There'd been so many misunderstandings and stupid secrets that, as far as he was concerned, they needed to counter it all with full-on transparency.

She looked at him and swallowed hard. "Of course it was Angus's words."

"That's what I don't know," Kascius admitted. "I need to get more information. What I want to do now is take you home and then get to the hospital to be with Liam. And, like it or not, I need to listen to whatever Angus has to say."

She sat back, her body now rigid, her fingers clenched. "You do that," she said in a formal tone. "I'll stay here with the lawyer, until he's done with this interview."

At that, Kascius turned to Larry. "Can you drive her home?"

He nodded. "I can do that. I need to talk to her sister anyway."

Ainsley frowned at Larry. "Why?"

He smiled. "We'll have to talk to everybody right now. Prepare yourself for a lot of questioning and a lot of doubts in the people around you."

"Why? Because two people I looked after both died?" she said bitterly. "I am a hospice nurse and have looked after people who were dying."

He nodded. "And potentially died by the same substance."

"That's terrible."

Kascius leaned over and gave her a hug. He brushed her cheek with a kiss. "I'll contact you as soon as I can, but I will sit with Liam for as long as he is at the hospital. So I may not get back to you today." And, with that, he disappeared, racing out to his vehicle and heading to his brother's side.

IT WAS A little worse than what he had told Ainsley.

Apparently Emily wasn't doing well, and the hemorrhaging would likely result in her going to surgery for an immediate C-section. When he reached the hospital, it didn't take much to find out where she was. As he got to the emergency room, Liam sat there, completely lost, staring at his hands in the waiting room. "How bad is it?" Kascius asked.

"Kascius." His brother bolted to his feet, as relief washed over his face. Kascius hugged him. "Dear God. To have made it this far—" Liam began.

"And she could still make it, but we've got to stay positive at this point."

He nodded. "That's what they said. The baby is still … *viable*, they called it. But, with the hemorrhaging, … they don't know. There's still a chance we could lose them both."

At that, Kascius winced. "Just hang tight. She's a strong woman, and you know she's fighting for that baby with everything she has. Just sit tight. We'll get news soon."

Liam looked over at him. "I don't think she believed it. I think she's so confused and shocked, you know?"

"It's understandable. I certainly don't believe Ainsley did anything to Mam."

"No, I don't think so either." Liam shook his head. "I don't know why the hell Angus would accuse her of such a thing right off the bat. God, I hate him right now."

"Because he's a troublemaking pain in the ass, and he always has been." Kascius felt the old anger chasing up inside him. "I'm also pretty sure he's the one who went to Dad and told him lies about me."

"What are you saying?"

"Someone, God knows who, told Dad that I planned to get the farm and to sell it as soon as I got it in my possession. After that, Dad never gave me a chance to even speak to him about it ever again."

At that, Liam stared at him. "Good God. Dad would have killed you over that."

"That's the problem. Instead of trusting me, or even having a conversation, he believed Angus—at least I think it was him, and that was the end of it. I don't know if there was anything else—or anyone else—who might have helped support that story or not."

"Such as Mam?" Liam suggested in a hard voice.

At that, Kascius nodded. "But I wasn't given a chance to counter the lies. They disowned me and made sure I would never have anything to do with the farm after that. The fact is, Dad didn't trust me or even give me a chance to defend myself. So I was found guilty, quartered, and hung without anyone else even knowing. And, with that happening so fast, it was pretty hard to even be part of the family much after that."

"Good God. How could you even stand to be around us? I didn't know any of that."

"No, of course you didn't. The trouble is, Angus could never get you away from being Dad's favorite. He was far too lazy for the farmwork that would have been required, so he went on to cultivate the next best thing, becoming Mam's favorite."

"Oh my God." Liam stared at the ceiling. "How could he even play games like that?"

"Because none of it mattered to him at all. What mattered to him was getting what he wanted. The trouble is, I never understood what he wanted. Was it just to play games with us, or did he really want the farm for himself? I think he just wanted to sell it, to take the money and run."

"I can see that part," Liam agreed. "He's often told me that, if I died, he would sell the place. Family lineage be damned. He doesn't want the farm, and I didn't really think that he would get it. But now to know that he'll get a part of it—" He shook his head at that thought. "And to buy him out would leave me with nothing to run the place on."

"I hear you. But we're not to that point yet."

"Yeah? Well, Mam's dead. And I can't even grieve the loss of my own mother because I'm ... in danger of losing my wife and my son," he whispered.

At that, Kascius leaned over and gripped his hand. "Keep the faith. Emily is strong. She's a fighter, and the two of you have fought so many battles. She's lost some, but she's also won so much, and we have to give her our strength and the faith that she can pull through this one too."

His brother looked over at him, gripped his hand hard. "They have to survive—or I'll have nothing left to live for."

CHAPTER 8

STILL IN SHOCK, Ainsley sat curled up on her couch, the reality of her world slowly settling in, as her sister Sibel sat beside her. Ainsley muttered, "I still can't believe this all happened so quickly."

"I don't know how it happened at all." Sibel stared at her curiously.

Ainsley shook her head. "It never occurred to me, in all my years of nursing, that I would ever be considered a murder suspect in the death of one of my patients," she whispered. She held out her shaky hands, watching them tremble, before clenching them together. "Look. The lawyer has been gone for hours, and I'm still sitting here, totally in shock."

"Sure you are," her sister said warmly. "This isn't anything you would have expected from that family you worked so hard for."

"Not the family," Ainsley snapped, her voice shaking with her surfacing anger. "I'll put the blame for this squarely on that asshole, Angus."

At that, her sister flushed.

Ainsley glared at her. "You've always defended him." Ainsley couldn't see why.

"That's right. I have. I can't believe he would have done what he did today."

But there was almost a hesitation in her voice. "You mean, without a good reason?" Ainsley shifted upward to stare at her sister in surprise. "Did you really think I would buy that you believe Angus would have done that without good reason or something behind his accusation?" Her voice rose into a crescendo.

Sibel stared at her, as if she'd gone mad. "I didn't say that. It's just not the Angus I know."

"Maybe you should tell me a little more about this Angus that *you* do know." She stared her sister in disbelief. "You know how I've felt about him all these years, and I thought you shared the same opinion."

"No." Sibel winced. "Not exactly."

As she stared at her sister, several things tumbled into place. "Good God." Ainsley gave a weary sigh, collapsing back. "You've had a crush on him too, didn't you?"

"It's hardly a crush when it's been there all these years." Sibel got up and put on the teakettle.

Ainsley struggled to process this information on her own. "And you never really saw that side to him? Or did you just ignore it?"

At that, her sister glared at her. "You know how hard it is when you care about somebody to see another side to them, particularly a negative side. It's not as if you were being terribly open and honest about your relationship with Kascius either."

"I wasn't hiding anything," Ainsley said bluntly. "We obviously had some issues."

"Yeah, including dating Angus, then rejecting him. Ever since then, he has pretty well hated you."

She stared at her sister. "Did you say, *hate?*"

"Yeah, *hate,*" Sibel leaned against the doorway frame.

"At least that's my take on it. And, because of his association with you, he won't have anything to do with me." Her sister walked back into the kitchen.

Ainsley wanted to call her back but didn't have a clue what she would say to her. The fact that her sister was hung up on somebody who was so different from anything good and healthy was stunning. As far as Ainsley could see, Angus had a plethora of issues, but Ainsley also felt terrible if her sister really cared about that asshole and felt as if everything in her life had stopped because of Ainsley's reactions to Angus.

When her sister walked back out later, it was obvious she'd been crying.

"Sibel, you know I didn't do anything to Angus, right?"

"You didn't have to." Sibel glared at her. "Once he got hung up on you, there was nobody else."

"That's BS," Ainsley protested. "He has dated a lot of women since then."

Her sister glared at her. "Oh, I know. Do you think I haven't seen or heard about every single one over these past few years?"

"He's always out with a new woman, it seems."

Sibel was crying openly now. "Exactly, but never me!" she snapped.

Ainsley didn't know what to say to that because there had to be a reason, but she also knew that there was absolutely nothing she could say to make her sister feel better about it. And when her sister saw her face, she nodded.

"I get it. He could have gone out with me, if he'd wanted to, and the fact is that he didn't. Because I remind him of you!" At that, her sister slumped down in an armchair.

"And none of it has anything to do with the nightmare

I'm currently going through? Right?" Ainsley laid on the couch to stare up at the ceiling.

"Don't go blaming Angus for that."

"No, of course not." Ainsley rolled her head to the side to stare at her sister in disbelief. "Why would I blame the man who accused me of killing his mother?"

"Obviously he was emotionally overwrought," Sibel said, with a wave of her hand.

That was the last straw for Ainsley. Her sister couldn't even acknowledge bad behavior from Angus. "What about your current boyfriend?"

"What about him? Of course I care about him," she said irritably, before Ainsley had a chance to say anything. "But it's not the same. Not compared to knowing that I wasn't acceptable all these years because of you. You made things so difficult, but I went out and tried to have a life anyway. Unlike you, who just sat here and did nothing but pout the whole time."

Ainsley winced at that because it was another direct hit, and one she hadn't expected. Normally the two of them were quite close, but, at the moment, her sister seemed to be holding inside a lot of resentment. So maybe they weren't as close as Ainsley had thought. On top of everything else, that made her even sadder. "Do you have any idea why Angus would have blamed me?" she asked cautiously.

Her sister snorted at that. "Because he believes it. He's not a liar, you know."

She didn't know what to say to that either. "So, do you believe his accusation as well?" she asked, her voice faint.

Her sister stared at her for a long moment. "No, ... I don't."

"Thank you for that," she muttered, closing her eyes in

relief. "It would be fairly distressing if my own sister thought I'd murdered a patient."

"I don't think you would. You're too high and mighty for that."

She winced at that. "Good God, Sibel. You know I'm hearing things right now that I really didn't need to hear. At least not from you."

"It's probably better that you do hear them." Her sister gave her a one-arm shrug. "You've always been very difficult to live with."

Ainsley didn't know what to say, as she stared at her sister. Finally she took a long deep breath. "How is it that you can feel that way and still live with me?"

"One has nothing to do with the other. We were left this house together, but you've got two-thirds, so it's not as if I have any say or can leave. I've got nowhere to go."

"Is that what you want to do?" She couldn't believe this conversation or the slow-building anger coming from her sister.

"Sure," she murmured. "It's not as if I want to stay here my whole life. But, if you won't sell, buy me out, or let me have the place, then what am I supposed to do?"

Once again, this seemed so wrong coming from her sister that Ainsley couldn't even think straight. She was too exhausted for this right now.

"Oh, give it a break," her sister muttered. "You're my sister, so I love you, of course, but it would have been nice if we could have sold this place, so I could have moved on. Yes, I've moved on in some ways but definitely not in others."

"Our mother left this house to all three of us," Ainsley whispered, feeling an unexpected heartache over just the mention of selling the house. "Leaving this house would feel like leaving Lanson."

"Lanson is dead," Sibel snapped. "I get that you want to keep some sort of a shrine in his honor, but you were also more than ready for him to die."

She winced at that, stunned. "Good God, Sibel. Is that what you really think?"

"That's what I know. Every day you were so upset that he was struggling and in so much pain, you wanted it over with."

"Sure, I wanted the pain he felt to be over with." She stared at her sister in horror.

At that, her sister waved her hand. "There wasn't anything anybody could do about it, was there? So he's better off dead."

And again, with this foreign nonsense coming out of her sister's mouth, Ainsley didn't even know what to say.

With a harrumph, her sister got up and flounced out of the room, leaving Ainsley shocked and staring into the darkness behind her, wondering what had just happened to her world.

Ainsley was exhausted and overwrought, but there was absolutely nothing going on right now that would give her the peace of mind required to break free enough to sleep. And yet she desperately needed sleep, before anything went even crazier in her world. She also had no idea what was going on with the rest of the family at the hospital with poor Emily.

Once the cops had taken Ainsley, she hadn't gotten any help or support from anyone, except Kascius. At least he had stepped up and had come immediately to her aid in a tangible way.

She wasn't at all surprised that her sister hadn't been

much help at the jail, yet Ainsley still reeled from their recent conversation. Typically, in times of trouble, Ainsley would have expected Liam and Emily to come to her aid, but then again, it was their mother Ainsley had just been accused of murdering. And now with Emily? ... Just thinking of her pregnant friend in the hospital, at risk of losing her baby and her own life, it brought tears to Ainsley's eyes all over again. She slowly got up, walking as if she were at least one hundred years old, as she made her way to her room. She ran a hot bath and soaked, trying to let some of the pain of the last few hours slide away.

It took several sleeping pills before she finally crashed.

WHEN AINSLEY WOKE up the next morning, it was too early to get up. As she remembered everything that had already happened, she closed her eyes and fell back to sleep again. When she woke later, with the sunlight streaming in, she realized the loud ringing of her phone had jolted her from sleep. She looked down at the number and answered. "Kascius," she said, her voice slurred.

"Are you all right?" he asked, his tone sharp.

"Yes, I woke up after a really bad night. Sleeping pills always leave me with a groggy head, and I'm not quite awake yet."

"I'm coming around to visit, so get up and put on the coffee." And, with that, he hung up.

She stared down at the phone, still disoriented and confused. But his tone was pretty firm. She got up and pulled on her robe, rather than getting dressed, then headed downstairs. She stumbled into the kitchen, hoping to find a pot of coffee, but there was no sign of it or her sister. Ainsley put on a fresh pot, and, as it was done dripping, Kascius drove up. As soon as he got to the front door, she was waiting for him. "So, what happened? Emily, is she okay? And the baby?"

He looked at her for a moment, then understanding crossed his face. "The baby was delivered by C-section late in the night, after Emily had hemorrhaged badly and was touch-and-go for some time. Both Emily and the baby boy are in critical condition right now."

Suddenly weak and dizzy, her strength reeling, the news was the last straw, and Ainsley collapsed.

KASCIUS CAUGHT AINSLEY before she landed on the floor, and he quickly moved her onto the couch. "Shit, I'm sorry," he whispered. "I should have prepared you better for that."

"They're both alive?" she whispered, when she could, her gaze searching his.

He nodded. "At the moment, yes. She lost an awful lot of blood, and the doctors think they've got it stopped now, but they don't know for sure yet. The baby is in intensive care in the neonatal unit."

She nodded slowly. "Good God, so what happened?"

"After the police led you away, I don't know exactly what happened. Angus was apparently there, and Emily contacted Liam, hysterical about the cops coming to get you and his mother being murdered. By the time he got there, she was on the floor, bleeding heavily."

"Oh my God," Ainsley cried out, trying to sit up, "and where the hell was Angus? Why didn't he help her?"

"I don't know. I haven't had a chance to connect with him. Apparently he went on a bender last night, and no one has seen him since."

"Jesus." She sagged onto the couch, brushing her hair off her face. "Trust him to be off on a bender, when the whole world has been torn apart, and people's lives are in chaos."

"He's caused a fair bit of damage to people with his lies and accusations. So I'm not against him staying away longer."

She nodded slowly. "Yeah, like me. And then, of course, my sister also hit me with a few extra blows last night. Nothing I would have expected in one million years."

"Like what?" he asked. She filled him in on the conversation and in all the ways she had apparently ruined her sister's life.

He stared at her. "That's a load of crock to blame you for all that."

She smiled weakly. "Thank you. It did feel very much as if I was thrown to the wolves, and nobody was there to save me." Then she hesitated and added, "Thank you for also not adding any of my list of faults."

"I don't like injustice, and nobody needs to be piling crap on anyone right now. You didn't kill your brother or my mother, and you certainly aren't responsible for your sister's happiness. I don't know what the hell is going on with Angus. As I said, he's gone underground. Yet why he's been such an ass now of all times? I don't know, except that it's very much classic Angus. It's anybody's guess at this point."

She gave a brief smile. "Whoever would have thought that my sister would be completely infatuated by him? She told me that Angus didn't lie and that she'd never seen anything other than a good side to him."

At that, Kascius winced. "That's very much a case of love being blind, isn't it?" He looked at her sharply. "Wait. I thought you mentioned that Sibel had somebody in her life."

"She does, but apparently she's been holding the torch for Angus all this time. Plus, according to her, Angus won't have anything to do with her because of me."

"So, why didn't you tell me whatever happened with you and Angus? When I left, you two seemed to be an item."

She stared at him in surprise, then shook her head violently. "Angus and I were never an item," she said flatly. "I made the terrible mistake of going out with him one time, and that was it. I flatly refused every time after that. He was far too much of a mouthpiece for me, so I told him that I didn't feel any connection and that I didn't want a relationship with him. I told him we could be friends, nothing more. He got angry about it and kept on trying. Relentlessly."

"*Nice.*" Kascius groaned. "He told me that you two were lovers and that you were getting married."

She stared at him, her jaw dropping. "Seriously?"

"Yeah, he sure did, and my mother also made a point of telling me that you would be a much better wife for Angus than me and that really I should get lost, so everybody's life would improve." He laughed, shaking his head. "When I look back on it, I wonder why I even stayed as long as I did. Liam and I were close, and I've always thought he and Emily were a great match. I was really happy for them, but, at some point in time, you have to cut your losses and go."

"My God." Ainsley sighed. "How can your family be such assholes?"

His grin flashed. "I think they come by it naturally."

"Apparently so, but that's no excuse."

"No, it's not an excuse, and they didn't need one. That's how they felt." Then he went on to explain what Angus had told his father about Kascius wanting to sell the farm, if he got it.

"So, that's why your dad kicked you out, isn't it?"

"Pretty much," he said cheerfully. "I don't blame them anymore really. By now I can see that leaving was the best thing for me in the end. Maybe not the best thing for Liam, but it was certainly the best thing for me."

"My God." Ainsley stared at him, trying to sort through the ripple effects from all the lies. "The thought of all that lying and troublemaking going on, it's unbelievable."

"I would have thought so, but apparently Angus is really good at it, and nobody seems to care."

"Do you know that every time he came to see Bella, he would say things like, 'What does the old bat want now?'" Ainsley shook her head. "Still, even after that, she adored him so much. I don't get it."

"Doesn't matter if we get it or not. The fact of the matter is that, as far as Mam was concerned, it was Angus or nobody."

"It's unbelievable," she whispered. "Scary even, when you think about it."

He shrugged. "I'm past it all."

"The cops are still looking at me though, right? I can't figure out what they think my motive would be. How on earth does that even begin to make sense in my world?"

"I'm not sure it does." He sighed. "I think somebody is out to cause you trouble."

"You mean Angus?"

He nodded. "That would make the most sense to me. He's clearly at it again."

"I don't get it. He could be doing so many things in life, and yet this is who he chooses to be?"

"It is, and it's not the easiest thing to understand, but my brother has always been a law unto himself, plus spoiled by my mother. The world was his, and all he had to do was take what he wanted. Honestly, Mam didn't care about Liam either."

Ainsley nodded. "With Bella gone, I'm afraid that's all Liam's problem now. I still don't understand the part about the property."

"I don't know either, as I've not been privy to any of it."

"Honestly, I don't want anything to do with any of it either. I presume there'll be an autopsy?"

"I would imagine so. I'll touch base with Larry in a little bit. I wanted to check in with you and to make sure you're okay, plus let you know about Emily. We can have a quick coffee, and then I'm off. I've got to go see the vet."

Her eyes lit up. "Did you find the War Dog?"

He nodded. "I did, but Beamer's in bad shape. Not as bad as another dog that was with Beamer though."

She winced, as he told her about it. "I have a yard here you can use, if you like."

He hesitated and then nodded. "Thanks. I'll see what Liam says first."

"Liam may not be in any shape to make decisions."

"Maybe not. I'll be there doing the chores, since he'll be at the hospital with Emily, so I could take the dogs there."

"Won't Angus be there?"

"I hope not." He groaned, with a heavy sigh. "If he is, it might be better to bring the dogs here, but is that going to cause a problem with your sister?"

She winced at that. "She's not anybody I even recognize

at the moment. This whole mess seems to have blown the lid off another big relationship issue I wasn't even aware of."

"Change does that, shock and change especially. In this case we'll get to the bottom of it." She hesitated, but he caught her expression. "Speak up. Something's on your mind."

"If it wasn't you, and it wasn't me …?"

He nodded. "Then who was it, right?"

She shrugged. "It's a natural-enough question."

"It is, and it's one we must get to the bottom of quickly. I don't even know what to say."

"Neither do I. It all seems so far-fetched."

"And yet it does appear to be what we'll have to deal with." He stood, tossing back his coffee. "Listen. Don't take any more sleeping pills."

"Why not? It's not as if I have anything else to do today."

"You could do with a rest after looking after my mother anyway. We don't want anybody, not your lawyer, the judge, or the police to conclude that you're a druggie and are dependent on such things to deal with obstacles in your life."

She stared at him, swallowed hard, "Right. So character will be everything because it's already been assassinated."

He winced. "That's one way to look at it."

As he got up to leave, she said, "Thank you."

"For what?" He looked at her curiously.

"For stepping up and being there for me. I have to admit that I was sitting in that jail, feeling let down and betrayed by Emily and Liam, but of course I didn't know she had collapsed."

"No, and I'm still trying to track down Angus. There was no sign of him this morning, and I presume last night he was probably out with his friends or at his place, but I don't know where he's at. I really don't want any trouble between him and Liam right now."

"Yet the minute there is a death, people start looking for their piece of the pie."

At that, Kascius nodded. "Exactly. I'll call you later." And, with that, he walked out the door.

As soon as he hopped into the truck, he phoned the vet to see if it was open, which it finally was.

"I'll be there in five minutes." He headed his vehicle in the direction of the vet's office. He wanted to take the injured dog out of there if he could, but, at the same time, he also knew that there might be some treatments potentially needed to stay in for. Beamer didn't look to be as badly injured as the other one, but he had no way of knowing for sure.

As soon as he pulled into the vet clinic and walked into the reception area, the vet stepped out to talk to him.

"So, Beamer is not in terrible shape. Obviously he is nutritionally deficient and struggling. He has some anxiety issues, possibly relating to abandonment. I'm not sure what's going on in his past history, but I don't have a problem letting you take him. He'll probably do better outside of this stressful environment. Now, the one that came in with him is another story."

"That one looked pretty badly injured when I brought the dog in. Will he make it?"

"Turns out she's female. Yeah, I think so, but it'll take some time. More important, she'll need some care."

"Right, I do have a place. A couple actually. My brother's farm for one, plus a friend has a large fenced area she offered as well."

The vet hesitated and then agreed. "Okay, sure, but not today. I've stitched up that nasty wound, and we've done X-rays. She's got a couple broken ribs, but it will take her a bit to get back outside again. Of course the behavioral issues are more of a problem in Beamer."

"Yeah, but I'm willing to take them both on. There's a reason why Beamer was connected to her, but I don't know whether it was because the dogfighting ring had them together at times or because he chose to be with her, but, when I saw them, he was standing protectively close to her—as close as he could with her in one pen and him in the other—and didn't want to let anybody near her."

"Yeah, we had that issue here as well."

It took a bit of finagling, but finally Kascius got the vet to agree that both dogs could come to him, but Kascius would only take the War Dog today. He worried that Beamer wouldn't be happy about leaving the other one behind, and that's exactly the way it turned out. He let Beamer sniff the other dog through the cage and then led him out to his truck.

Kascius would try Beamer at the farm first and see how that worked out, but, if Angus would cause trouble, Kascius would immediately take Beamer over to Ainsley's place. Now, if Ainsley's sister would cause a problem, well, he wasn't sure what he would do after that. Beamer needed somebody, and he needed somebody who was solid and dependable. The last thing they needed was more trouble. As he headed toward the farm, he called Liam. "Hey, where are you?"

"I'm still at the hospital." His tone was grim.

"Okay. Listen. I've got the War Dog, and I'm heading back to your place. Is that all right?"

"Yeah, sure, that's fine," his brother said. "I've got to head home and do the chores soon."

"I'm not sure what's on tap right now," Kascius said, "but I fed everybody and moved out another round bale of hay. Just tell me what else I need to do, and I'm all over it."

There was silence at the other end, and then his brother softly whispered, "Thank you. That means a lot."

"Dude, I could spend a lifetime here," he said, with a laugh. "I can feed horses and move cows and run tractors as I need to, but I don't know where you're at with any of it. So I'd probably do you more good if I had some direction from you, where I end up doing what you need me to do, instead of me making it up as I go along, you know?"

"I hear you. I was hoping she'd wake up, and I could talk to her first."

"I'm sure she'll wake up soon, but it might be worth checking to see if the doctors are keeping her sedated."

"They have been and are backing off that now." He hesitated. "Maybe I should come home."

"No, stay there with your wife for now. She needs to see you first thing when she wakes up. Just tell me what I need to do, and, when I get home with the War Dog, I'll run out and do the chores. Or more chores." He laughed. "There's never any end to them, is there?"

"No, there sure isn't."

"I haven't had any contact with Angus. Have you?"

"No, I haven't, and, after all the chaos he caused with his accusations, I'm not sure I even want to."

"No, I hear you."

At that, his brother hesitated. "Do you think there's any truth to the accusations?"

"No, I sure don't," Kascius declared cheerfully. "I think

he's being a disruptive shit, as always."

"But why?"

"I have one idea," he stated, as he told him about the conversation between Ainsley and her sister.

"Good God," Liam said. "So he's waited all this time to get back at Ainsley?"

"Maybe. It sounds strange and stupid, but you know it's possible."

"Right. It's not what you and I would do, but you can never tell about Angus."

"Apparently he also didn't have a whole lot of patience for Mam either."

"No, he used to say awful things every time he walked into the house. Always talking about the old bat and saying he couldn't wait until she was gone, so he could get his money."

"Is there any money?" Kascius asked.

"I don't even know. I don't know if Mam changed her will or whatever it was in the first place. I don't know anything you could hang your hat on." Liam groaned. "I need to contact Mam's lawyer and find out."

"I'm almost to the house. I think I'll go take a look closer in her room."

At that, his brother hesitated. "Do you really think something is going on here?"

"I don't know, Liam, but I don't like any of this. It's completely ruined Ainsley's world and her reputation, which is totally unnecessary, but whether it's just petty differences or something more, I don't know. I'll take Beamer in anyway and see if we've got something to feed him. Otherwise I'll need to get dog food."

"I can do that on the way home, if need be," his brother

offered. "I'll give Emily the morning to wake up and to see me, and then maybe I'll come on home and do something useful this afternoon."

"Only if you want to," Kascius replied. "Otherwise you stay there. She's the most important thing right now, and I've got this." With that, he hung up.

As he pulled into the driveway, there was no sign of Angus, and a part of Kascius was relieved.

It would be a hell of a scene when they did meet. But he also needed to be a little calmer and in a better space to deal with his brother's lies and to see if he had any motive more plausible than just an unrequited love. Kascius found that very hard to believe, since his brother had been very active with untold women all these years.

Besides, as far as he could tell, Angus could only love himself.

Kascius highly doubted that Angus held a torch for Ainsley. If anything, it sounded more like a case of revenge for having rejected him. That sounded much more likely. Kascius let Beamer out, spending a few minutes to scratch and rub his back.

"I know, boy," he said, as the War Dog watched him warily. "It's been a shit deal for you, hasn't it?" He looked around the house, before turning toward Beamer again. "But we're getting there, honest to God. I know it seems as if you've been treated pretty rough so far, but hopefully that's over with."

Beamer woofed in agreement.

Kascius couldn't even imagine a family not wanting this War Dog. What the hell was wrong with people? Sure, Beamer was probably a handful, and that was something Kascius might need somebody to look at. Maybe Beamer wasn't ready to be released to the general public.

It sure as hell wasn't the War Dog's fault. As Kascius headed inside, he looked around and realized that everything had been left as it was. He groaned as he saw the blood everywhere. "We'll have to clean this up." With the War Dog safely inside, Kascius took off Beamer's leash and locked the door, so that Angus couldn't come in suddenly and spook Beamer, ruining whatever relationship Kascius had begun to build with the dog. He grabbed some old towels from the utility room and headed toward the bloodstains.

The War Dog sniffed at his side but didn't seem to be too bothered. He raced around the living room and the kitchen area, whining.

The trouble was, people heard *War Dog*, and they thought *tough*. They didn't see a dog that had already been to the war and beyond, and, in this case, they probably just saw money. But, as far as Kascius was concerned, some of these War Dogs would make absolutely fantastic therapy dogs.

Maybe that was something he should consider. It's not that Kascius had that training, but he sure as hell had experience, and it wouldn't take very much to make these dogs great friends and pets for people who needed them. These dogs were used to working. They loved—no, needed—a purpose. It was a matter of having a place of his own. It came back to the fact that Liam had the farm, and Kascius didn't have his own place. Even Sibel and Ainsley had a house together. And considering that Ainsley had devoted years without pay or another job to Lanson's care, it wouldn't have surprised him if Lanson had left his part of the property to her. He didn't know what Sibel would think of such a thing, but then nobody seemed to know what Sibel was thinking these days.

After he had cleaned up the blood and the scattered trash from the paramedics coming to get Emily, plus all the other signs of distress that had gone on, Kascius slowly walked to Mam's room and threw the bedroom door open wide.

His eyebrows shot up. The bedroom had been completely destroyed, with the bedding on the floor, sheets and pillows everywhere, night table drawers opened and dumped. He wasn't exactly sure what the hell he was looking at. He took several photos and sent them to Liam, asking if this is what he would have expected the room to look like.

Liam phoned immediately. "Hell no," he cried out. "What the hell happened there?"

"I don't know," Kascius said honestly, still looking around the room. "I got home and cleaned up all the blood out in the living room and set that room to rights. It was a mess that I didn't want you to come home to. Then I went to Mam's room, and this is it. I'm not even sure what to think."

"Neither am I. But considering how wrecked it is, maybe call the cops."

Kascius thought about it and agreed. "You're right. That's exactly what I should do." He hung up and quickly phoned the detective that he'd spoken to at the station. Then he phoned the lawyer, Larry.

As soon as everybody had been informed, the lawyer responded, "I'm on my way over. I want to take a look at this place." And, with that, he hung up. Larry got there at the same time as the cops. The cops didn't appear to be happy to see him, but Larry shrugged and stood his ground. "Hey, you've accused an innocent woman, so anything that's to the contrary is something I need to see."

The cops didn't say anything more to that. But, as they stepped in and looked around at the room, one said, "How do we know you didn't do this?"

Kascius stared at him. "You don't, do you? But I can tell you that I came from picking up Beamer at the vet's. Then I cleaned up all the bloodstains out there from Emily's collapse. Afterward I came in here to find the room like this."

"What possible reason would anybody have for doing this?"

The lawyer immediately spoke up. "Seems someone was looking for something to me." He turned and looked at Kascius. "Any idea what?"

He shrugged. "No, Mam has always lived here, but is now more or less bed ridden. I don't even really know at what point in time she was moved downstairs to this room but as her ability to handle the stairs declined, it was deemed safer to shift her down here. But it's not as if she hasn't been sleeping most of the time. Anybody could have searched at any time really. But this?" He waved an arm. "Why this level of destruction? I really don't know what the hell is going on here right now. This is something I was hoping you guys could sort out."

"We will," the detective said. "Although it may not go the way you thought it would."

"I'm used to that," Kascius replied. "I've spent a lot of time in the military doing operations overseas, and, when life blows up, it tends to do it in a big way."

The detective nodded. "Just don't get in our way."

"I don't have any intention of getting in your way." Kascius gazed at him with a hard glint. "But neither do I have any intention of letting you railroad somebody who spent years devoted to caring for my mother. If you accuse Ainsley of murder out of the blue, you better have hard evidence and none of that circumstantial bullshit."

"I guess the question here is," Larry interrupted cautiously, "what possible motive would she have?"

"I don't think the police are thinking about a motive at all," Kascius said briskly. "Just wants somebody to accuse, so they can move on to the next case."

"That's not true," the detective protested. "We weren't the original accusers."

"No, but you sure picked that up. Did you ever consider that maybe the person doing the accusing is the one who did the crime?"

"What motive would he have?" The detective looked directly at him.

"Why are you so concerned about a motive now that we're talking about my brother? You guys didn't give a crap about a motive when you arrested Ainsley." He noticed the cops glancing at the War Dog several times, even though he was leashed. Then Beamer nudged his leg.

"He seems pretty calm," the detective noted cautiously.

"Yeah, he's upset because he's missing that other dog he was so protective of, but I've not yet seen any negative behaviors from him."

"That's good news. I don't know what skills he's got, but maybe you can put them to good use."

"Possibly," Kascius agreed. "I have to clarify his health first and then check out his training."

The cop nodded at that. "As I said before, we always have a need for your skills and his."

Kascius nodded. "And I'll consider it. However, I've got other things to deal with for now."

The cop looked around at the scene. "It looks to me as if somebody was looking for something and got pissed off. This is about rage." He turned to Kascius and asked, "Who would that be?"

"I have no idea, but I can tell you that it wasn't Ainsley."

"Yet we don't know that for sure, do we?"

Kascius frowned. "I visited her yesterday morning in the jail, and the lawyer was there to get her out on bail. Her sister was with her through the night, until Sibel went to work this morning."

"But we don't even know when this happened in your mother's room, do we?" the cop asked.

"No, I guess we don't."

The conversation died, as everybody studied the area.

"I've got a question for you," the detective said, turning to look at him.

"What's that?"

"Who inherits?"

He was caught by surprise and then nodded. "That's funny. We've been talking about that among ourselves."

"Talking about what?"

"We have no proof of who inherits what. We believe that our mother's share of the farm will go to my youngest brother, Angus. That's what we were all told years ago, but I don't know if that's true or if it may have changed in the years since."

"Wait, so Liam doesn't own the farm outright?"

"Our mother and Liam held joint ownership. Liam has three-quarters, and she had one-quarter."

"Interesting, but not really a compelling motive."

"No, not that I know of, and I really don't see any reason at all for someone to have knocked her off early." He winced at his own phrasing. "I don't mean that to sound insensitive, but, when it comes to my mother, she was a force unto herself."

"I think they can get a whole lot worse as they get to that stage of life too," the detective agreed, with a nod. "But obviously there was no love lost between the two of you."

"Not particularly." Kascius gave a cheerful smile. "She hated the sight of me. But, on the other hand, I love my brother Liam, and I am much less close to Angus. All of that will come out once you start questioning us, so I have absolutely no problem sharing."

"And you're here for the War Dog."

"I'm here for the War Dog and to visit my brother Liam and his wife." At that, his smile fell away. "Who even now is in the hospital, fighting for her life from whatever the hell happened yesterday."

At that the detective turned, looked at him in surprise. "What do you mean? I heard she fainted or something. Are you saying it was worse than that?"

Kascius snorted. "Yeah, quite a bit worse. She hemorrhaged, and they had to deliver the baby by C-section late last night. Mother and babe are both in intensive care and not out of the woods by any means."

At that, the detective frowned. "I'm sorry to hear that. I don't know how we managed to not leave any notes about that." He frowned again, as he looked at his phone. "Damn, that is something I would have liked to have known sooner."

"Yeah, you're not kidding. The arresting officers were probably so happy to arrest Ainsley that they didn't bother to check things out with the other people who actually live here. Now that you know my middle brother is at the hospital, you can talk to him when necessary."

"Everybody will need to be questioned," the detective agreed in a calm voice.

"Understood. Anyway, I'm filling in for Liam here on the farm, so I need to go out and take care of chores. Can I leave you guys to it?" With that, he stepped through the bedroom door into the hallway, Beamer by his side. "Come on, boy. We have things that need to get done."

Just then came a shout from the front door. He groaned and stepped back inside Mam's room. "That would be Angus."

Angus walked into the living room, glaring at everybody. "What the hell is going on?" But before anybody had a chance to react, Beamer, who'd been quite sedate until this point in time, lunged at Angus, dragging the leash away from Kascius. He leapt forward and grabbed it before Beamer reached his brother.

Angus cried out and stepped back. "Jesus Christ," he cried out in fear. "What the hell is a killer dog doing in here?"

At that, the cop looked over at Kascius. "You've got to keep him under control."

"He *is* under control." Kascius held back Beamer, even now snarling at the new arrival. Kascius stared at his baby brother. "I can't help but wonder what made him react that way to Angus in the first place."

CHAPTER 9

AINSLEY WONDERED WHETHER it was safe to call the hospital or at least call Liam for an update. She was working up the courage when Larry called.

"Have you been over to Bella's house at all?"

"No, of course not. Why would I even want to go there?"

"Is there anybody who can vouch that you've been at home?"

"Potentially," she said cautiously, "but Kascius left a little while ago."

"He's the one who called me in. Bella's bedroom has been tossed, and they're looking to see who would have done it."

"So, I suppose because I don't have anybody who can say I didn't do it, that makes me the likely suspect," she said bitterly.

"That's one part of it, but, outside of Liam, who was at the hospital all night—"

She winced at that reminder. "Of course he was. God, I was wondering if it was okay to go to the hospital and to see how Emily's doing, but then I thought about what reaction I might get and chickened out. I was trying to get my courage up to call him."

"Let me talk to him first," her lawyer said. "I'm looking

for an update on Emily as it is."

"Right. I wouldn't want to intrude on that either. But Emily is my best friend, so I'm ready to do anything I can to help."

"I'll pass on that message. I'll also tell them that it's been my recommendation that you not contact them."

"I would appreciate that," she whispered. "Lord knows I want to."

"I get that, and we'll get there. But, at the moment, the cops are trying to figure out why Bella's room would have been tossed."

"I don't know. Her medications were there, but I always left them in the same place, up until I thought that something could be going on, and then I moved them."

"Where did you move them to?" he asked immediately.

"There's a series of drawers in the bathroom. I put them in the back of the top drawer on the left."

"Any particular reason you put them there?"

"Because it's so far in the back that, unless you were looking for them, you couldn't tell they were there."

He hesitated at that. "You really were worried that something was going on."

"Yes, and with good reason apparently."

After that, he hung up, leaving her staring down at her phone in confusion. Why on earth would somebody toss Bella's room? It didn't make any sense to her. It's not as if anything was hidden. She frowned, thought about it, and then she remembered. She snatched her phone and, when the lawyer answered, spoke immediately. "Her journals. Bella's journals were there."

"Were where?"

"In her bedroom."

"Where would she have put them? What was in them?"

"I don't know. I would guess anything from her deluded ramblings to nasty comments about her sons, but honestly, I don't know. Bella was a lovely person mostly, when you kept the conversation away from family issues, and she would sometimes talk for hours and sounded almost sane. Once the topic of family entered the discussion, she tended to run off the rails."

"What do you know about Kascius and the family?"

"That Kascius has been poorly treated by almost everybody in the family." She gave him some explanation and told him what she could, without going too far, since it wasn't her story to tell.

He swore. "Good God, and that was Angus."

"Yes, that was Angus, but you'll have to talk to him."

"He's here now, so we will talk with him." With that, he hung up again.

Ainsley couldn't get warm. She paced back and forth, and in between she made herself more tea, paced some more, and then made more tea. When still she had no answers or updates from anybody, she phoned Kascius. As soon as he answered, she snapped, "Did anything change?"

"What's to change?" he asked curiously.

"I don't know," she cried out. "The lawyer called me and asked me a bunch of questions about Bella's room."

"I'm sure he did." Kascius's tone was calm, steady. "I'm out of the loop because I'm outside working on chores."

She stopped. "Good God, I didn't even think of all that. I was trying to figure out why nobody had updated me or had given me any indication of what was going on."

"There'll be a lot of that for a while. Remember. You didn't do anything, and there's absolutely no reason to be worried."

"Yeah, except for the part about being arrested and held on suspicion of murder."

"But they released you," he said, "and no charges have been filed yet."

"Sure, but it'll happen. You know that."

"We don't know that, so let's focus on things we can do something about."

She stopped and looked down at her phone. "Do what though? And when you say chores, do you have an update on Emily?"

"I haven't talked to Liam in the last little bit. He's staying at the hospital, and Emily is still sleeping. She isn't out of the woods, and I told him that I would cover chores, so he could stay there because that's where he needs to be. Therefore, I don't really have much for you. Now I'm thinking I want to see him come home for a bit, so I can get some rest."

"I asked the lawyer to let me know if I could go to the hospital and see him and Emily and the baby. Do you think he ..." Then she stopped, unable to say it.

"Liam doesn't blame you," Kascius said gently. "However, I'm not sure the hospital is where you need to be right now."

"Sitting here and doing nothing is driving me batty," she snapped. "Not only was I working every day, looking after your mother, but now everything has blown up in my face, and I'm really struggling."

"As soon as I'm done with this, I'll run by the hospital. I'll let you know as soon as I learn something."

"Which isn't the same thing as me going to the hospital," she murmured in a wry tone.

"No, it isn't, but, if your lawyer suggests that you don't

go right now, then don't. There's a reason we hire these guys. They know the best answers at the moment, and they are able to be more objective."

"Maybe so, but all this is driving me crazy."

"I get it. I do. Listen. You can probably phone the hospital and ask a nurse for an update on Emily without anybody getting upset. With privacy laws, they can't say much, so it won't be a detailed report of course, but better than nothing. Please, avoid going there, okay?" And, with that, he said, "I've got to get back to work. I've got Beamer here. Oh, let me ask you this. Have you ever seen Angus around dogs?"

"No, not that I can recall. Why?"

"Because this War Dog went absolutely nuts when he saw him and not in a good way."

She gasped. "What?"

"Yeah. I had a hard time pulling him back. It sucks too because now the cops think Beamer is more dangerous than he seemed before."

"Oh my God. Do you think the War Dog is dangerous?"

"I would have said no, before seeing him jump at Angus, but every animal is dangerous in the wrong circumstances. I need to find out more history on Beamer, such as his training and service record."

"What wrong circumstances are you talking about?"

He went silent, then added, "Let me think about that a little. Call you later." And, with that, he hung up.

She sat back down on the couch and waited. When the lawyer called ten minutes later, he shared, "I've spoken to Liam, and you're welcome to go to the hospital. However, he also told me that there's absolutely no reason to visit right now because Emily's sleeping anyway, and you would have to stay in the waiting room. With the baby in the neonatal ICU, no one can see him. Plus Liam is sitting at Emily's side."

"Right, so not much point." Ainsley groaned. "Good Lord, what a mess."

"It is a mess, but, at the same time, we're getting somewhere at least."

"Says you, but I'm the one sitting here on suspicion of murder."

"I don't expect it'll be that way for long. They're looking for the journals, but they haven't found them."

"Bella was a bit paranoid at times and had a habit of hiding them."

"I thought she was bedridden."

"She was. Not very often or very well, but she was somewhat mobile." Ainsley hesitated. "She was fragile. And a very odd lady at times," she offered, for lack of a better word. "She did things sometimes that didn't make any sense to me. Yet other times, she seemed to have complete clarity. She was always somewhere between those two extremes, and I was left to figure which state she was in from one moment to the next."

"Right. So sometimes she was herself, and sometimes she wasn't. Is that what you're trying to say?"

"Most of the time, she was herself, with the confusion or lapses you would expect from someone her age and in her condition. But, every once in a while, there would be an odd reference, and I wouldn't have a clue to what she was talking about. I didn't know whether it was something she was trying to be secretive about or something else entirely. I just don't know."

"Right, I'll call you when I know more."

She immediately phoned Liam. "Liam," she cried out, when he answered. "I'm so sorry. My God, how is Emily now?"

"Emily is holding on," he said, his tone warming with the better news. "The doctors are optimistic."

"Thank heavens for that," she murmured. "I'm so sorry I can't come in and sit with her."

"Hey, I understand. It sounds as if you're better off to stay where you are until this nightmare is sorted out."

"Yeah, assuming that it gets sorted out," she said, with a bitterness that was almost crazy to her. "I can't believe this is happening."

"No. I can't either. I'm sorry I can't be there to help sort it out. At the moment, I'm caught up in this hospital."

"I know. ... Look. I guess you've talked to the lawyer, but I can't think of any reason why your mother's room would have been ransacked, can you?"

"No, no idea," he replied. "And honestly, her room seems not even important right now, when I look at what I'm dealing with here."

She immediately winced. "And you're right. I shouldn't have even brought it up. I'm sorry."

"No, no, no, that's not what I meant." Liam took a deep breath. "Anything that helps clear your name is important. I didn't mean it that way. It's just that it's hard for me to focus on anything else but Emily and the baby. However, Emily is holding on. Just the fact that she's even alive is something I'm so grateful for right now. It's been a nightmare. We need to get your nightmare cleared too."

"Do you have any idea why your brother would have accused me of that?"

"Angus? No, unless it's ancient anger over you ditching

him way back when."

She stared at the phone. "Did you know about that?"

"Sure. At the time, he was pretty angry about it all. For a while, he didn't have anything nice to say about you, but I put it down to you not being ready to give up on Kascius."

She shook her head at that. "I didn't realize that you even knew."

"Most of us did," he said, his tone wry. "It's a small town, and we're all family."

"It never even occurred to me that it was an issue."

"It shouldn't be an issue. You're entitled to have whatever feelings you have."

"Yet somehow it doesn't feel like that," she said sadly. "I didn't even realize how upset I was when Kascius left. I just got really angry."

"Yeah, well, Kascius had a lot of anger in him as well, and honestly, most of it was very justified about our family. I didn't even realize everything that had gone on back then, and it makes me pretty angry now for him. It's a wonder he ever came back at all."

"I know, and that's just the little bit I've heard about. But he has handled it, and he's come back a much better man."

"Except for his disability, which is why he thinks you don't want anything to do with him."

She gasped. "Disability?"

Silence came first. "Oh Jesus." The words exploded from Liam's mouth. "I didn't expect to be the one to tell you. I thought it was obvious. And it never mattered to me, so … damn. Look. Forget I said anything, okay? Oh, here's the doc. I've got to run." And, with that excuse, he quickly rang off.

She stood, staring down at the phone. "Good Lord, what the hell was that all about?" She wanted to rush to the hospital and brace Liam, but he obviously felt very uncomfortable even talking about it. Yet Kascius hadn't mentioned it at all. Of course she was sensitive about military disabilities because that was the cause of her brother's pain. The nerves never died off from his leg, and he had suffered with phantom pain constantly. That was something that most people didn't talk about, but, for her brother, that pain, along with constant infections, had been traumatizing for him. She wanted to phone Kascius, yet didn't even know what to say. It's not as if she could call out of the blue and ask him about the nature of the disability he had failed to mention.

Oh my God, was that what the cryptic message from Emily had been about? Kascius's disability? Oh my God.

Ainsley thought about the times she had seen Kascius in the last few days and did recall picking up a bit of a limp once in a while. She had attributed it to a sore leg, thinking maybe he had banged himself, as she was doing all the time. She sat here, deep in thought, but didn't have any place to go.

When the door opened, and her sister walked in, Sibel looked at her and rolled her eyes. "Gee, I thought you'd be at the hospital."

"My lawyer suggested it was better if I didn't go just yet."

"Why not, unless they think that you hit Emily too."

At that, Ainsley gasped.

Her sister waved her hand. "Oh, never mind. I was trying to lighten the mood, which was obviously ill-advised." And with that she stalked into the kitchen.

Ainsley stared behind her. Is that really what her sister was joking about? How could anybody find anything along that line worth laughing about? But, as she sat here, she realized there was an awful lot going on in her sister's head that Ainsley didn't recognize. Knowing it would get ugly, she finally stepped into the kitchen. "Do you want to explain what's going on?"

Sibel looked over at her, then shrugged. "Not really."

"I would appreciate it if you would. I really don't understand."

"How could you not understand? It was bad enough that you were sitting home on your backside, nursing our brother, while I worked my ass off, trying to support all three of us, but then to find out that he had left you his part of the house was too damn much. So, even though I need the money, I need to get out of this house so I can move on and have a life of my own. Yet I can't because you don't want to sell, and you don't have the money to buy me out. So, I'm stuck living here, even though it's the last place I want to be. As always, everything comes down to whatever falls within your little bubble, with no thought about anybody but yourself!" And, with that, Sibel darted out of the kitchen and up to her room. "God, I hate this place, and, for that matter, I fucking hate you too."

Then Sibel's bedroom door slammed hard as Ainsley stood here, dumbfounded.

AS KASCIUS WALKED, he reviewed some training with Beamer, who seemed to have lightened up ever-so-slightly. He was walking with his head up, checking out his surroundings, and appeared to be a little more comfortable. Kascius patted Beamer several times. "It's okay, boy. I know you don't understand what's happened to your world. It's been flipped way too many times to be comfortable. I really wish you could tell me why you reacted like that to my brother though."

Kascius's immediate thought was pretty ugly, and he didn't understand if that was even possible. But he really knew nothing about his brother these days. He finished feeding the horses, then checked on the rest of the animals. Liam would likely come home today. Even though Kascius didn't know when, he still wanted to get the chores done. Kascius wanted to help as much as he could.

He quickly moved through the rest of the chores and then went back to the house. To his surprise, nobody was there. Angus was gone, and so were the cops. Wondering at that, Kascius checked through the kitchen and the rest of the rooms, but he saw no sign of the cops, his brother, no one.

He picked up his phone and made a call, and the minute he heard Liam's voice, he smiled. "Wow, you sound better. What's happening?"

"She's awake," he cried in joy. "She's doing better."

"Thank God." Kascius laughed in relief. "Damn. That's great news. I'm so happy to hear it."

"Yeah, me too. I'm heading to the car right now. She basically sent me home, and the baby is doing much better too," he added, chuckling. "Told me to get my ass back here and take care of things."

"Yeah, that sounds like Emily." Kascius grinned. Damn this was great news. "Not sure there's a whole lot you need to take care of though. But get home anyway, as you probably need a shower at least and some sleep. I've done the bulk of the chores, but I'm not sure what I might be missing."

"That's fine. I'll figure it out when I get there. I really appreciate the help."

"That's what family is for." Hanging up the phone, Kascius walked back into the kitchen and put on a pot of coffee. Knowing that Liam would be home soon was even more of an impetus to put on the coffee. Kascius's heart was light, as he realized there was actually some good news from the hospital.

He phoned Ainsley to give her an update, but, when he found it was busy, he quickly sent her a text with the news. Next, he intended to contact Angus, but, for whatever reason, he held off. He walked back into his mother's room, wondering what the hell anybody could have been looking for. Ainsley had told the lawyer about the journals, but Kascius didn't know anything about why or where she would have even hidden them.

Given her state of mind toward the end, he was willing to go with the reality that she was having more trouble navigating life in general. And that made him sad. He didn't know precisely when she became so difficult about things, but it made him wonder what the options were when you got older. Did everyone have to go through the same craziness that she had?

By the time the coffee was done dripping, he poured a cup and poked around in the fridge, looking for something to make for dinner. When his phone rang, it was Ainsley. "Hey, you didn't have to call. I just wanted to give you an update. Emily is awake and doing much better, and Liam is on his way home for a bit."

"Good," she cried out, and he heard the tears of joy in her voice. "I'm so glad to hear that."

"Yeah, me too. Everything is a shitstorm right now."

"Yeah, you're not kidding. I'm still waiting to hear back from the lawyer. Do you know if they found Bella's journals?"

"No idea, though I don't even know why anybody would care."

"I don't know why, but there were times that she would write in them. Maybe something she wrote in them is something that someone doesn't want anyone to see."

He hesitated at that. "Is there something you're trying to tell me?"

"No. Is there something you need to tell me?"

He stared at his phone, surprised. "No. I don't know why you would say that or what I would need to tell you."

She hesitated. "Okay, but I think we need to have another talk."

"Sure, I'm okay to talk. If you want to come on over, feel free. Liam is on his way home though, if that matters to you."

"I don't know. Maybe I won't then," she said nervously. "I don't know what kind of reaction I'll get from him. I did call him at the hospital though, and he seemed to be okay when we spoke but …"

"I'm sure he's fine. Anyway, I'll leave that up to you. I'll throw some dinner together right now, so there's something for him to eat. I'm guessing he hasn't eaten or slept." And, with that, he rang off, not really giving her much of a chance to argue.

He had no clue what Ainsley was talking about, but she would share when she was ready. So he went into the kitchen and grabbed some hamburger and started frying it, as he prepped the with onions and celery. Beamer lay on the floor, just barely out of the way, watching him intently. Dog food was on his list of supplies to get immediately. However, tonight Beamer was probably eating whatever they were. Looking around to see what ingredients he had to work with, he was thinking about tacos. As he looked through the cupboards, he kept wondering about those damn journals.

Ainsley had put that note of suspicion in his mind, and it wasn't likely to go away now. But where could his mother have even hidden them? And had whoever trashed the room found them and taken them away? All this fuss really made no sense because there was really just the four of them with access to Mam and her room, other than Ainsley. His brothers and Emily. He couldn't think Emily or Liam would do that, but it was also just way too easy to assume that it was Angus. By the time Kascius had fried his mind on the topic, he remembered the hamburger, and thankfully it was still in pretty good shape.

He pulled some off to a plate to cool, for Beamer later. Adding in the onions, he sauteed those until translucent then added celery, tomatoes and Italian seasoning for a spaghetti sauce, then put a big pot of water on to boil for pasta. As soon as everything was at a point that he could leave it simmering on the stove, he headed to his mother's bedroom, Beamer at his side.

Kascius stopped in the middle of the room and stared at it first from the perspective of what Mam would be trying to hide—a journal, something maybe 5x8 inches. Then, second, if she really were trying to hide a small journal, what would she have access to from her bed, so that she didn't have to get up on her own? Third, where could she hide such a journal pretty fast, before anybody else could find them? And, with those three considerations in mind, he looked around the room carefully.

There were several dresser drawers still on the floor, but he presumed that the cops had taken a closer look there. So, if anything had been there, they should have found it. He steadily kept going through the room, always thinking from Mam's perspective as to where she might have hidden the journals. Beamer sniffed the bottom drawer of one of the two nightstands and whined. Since those drawers had already been emptied, with a sudden understanding, Kascius pulled out the bottom drawer completely and got down on his hands and knees to check behind the drawer. Sure enough, in the back, was a small black hardcover book.

It was stuck there and so took a bit to pull it out, but, once he had it free, he flipped it open and nodded. "That's exactly what I was looking for."

Then Beamer growled. Kascius froze, already knowing who to expect.

"It's what everybody else was looking for too apparently," said a man from the doorway.

"Seems to be," Kascius replied, identifying the voice immediately.

"It figures that you would be the one to find it."

Kascius turned slowly to stare at his baby brother and the gun in his hand. "Jesus, seriously, Angus? You know that's almost too cliché."

"I didn't kill her." Angus laughed.

"Yeah, sure you didn't."

"No, I didn't have to."

He stared at his baby brother. "What are you talking about?"

"Oh, that's right. You don't know anything. You weren't here for all these years while she was fading. God, that was painful."

"So, you're saying you didn't do anything to help her along?"

"Nope. I didn't have to." He smiled slyly. "It was even better than that."

Not sure what Angus meant, Kascius hoped he could keep his youngest brother talking.

But, when Angus stepped closer, one hand out, Beamer let out a howl from deep in the back of his throat.

Angus froze. "You'll need to give me that book."

"Why?" Kascius held it out of reach.

"Do you see the gun? No way in hell you'll stop me. And not only are you—you know—supremely broken, and, if you think I won't put a bullet in that dog's head, you're wrong." He snickered. "You don't even want the farm now. Isn't that too funny? You know, in the end, Dad was changing his mind about you, thinking it might end up being the making of the man, so to speak."

Kascius stared at him. "I doubt it. He was pretty stuck on the fact that I was walking away from the farm."

"That is true, and I did my best to feed that. But, at the end of the day, I think Dad was going to turn the farm back over to you."

Kascius stared at him, as he got a horrible sinking feeling in his stomach. How far would Angus go? "Did you kill him?"

Angus stared at him. "Wow, that's a stretch, isn't it? I tell you that Dad was changing his mind about the farm, and you suddenly assume a man dying of natural causes was murdered? *Huh.*"

Kascius stared at Angus, hating the suspicion he felt, yet no longer able to think of anything else. "So, are you going to tell me or not?"

"No, surely not." Angus laughed. "Somebody like you? Chances are you've got some secret listening device on you."

As it was, he had his phone in his hand, the video and audio already recording. "Yeah, right. I'm such a modern hi-tech guy." Kascius laughed. "So, what the hell? Do you really mean Dad was changing his mind?"

"You heard me. He seemed to get soft in his old age. Mam was getting pretty upset about it too."

"What do you mean? Was she was changing her mind too? I'm starting to think this is all bullshit."

"No, she was pissed off that Dad was changing his mind. She didn't want you to have anything to do with the place."

"No, she only wanted you to have it, I suppose. Right?"

"Absolutely," Angus confirmed, with a smile. "And she was getting angrier and angrier that she couldn't fix it. But she did it. She found a way. You know that, right?"

"What do you mean, Angus?"

"She did fix it. She fixed it so the farm becomes mine."

"How can that be? Three-quarters is Liam's," he stated, staring at his brother in astonishment. "And why would she even care? They looked after her all these years."

"They also paid your lovely girlfriend's bills for her too. But I figured that, in the end, we'd get her pretty good too."

"Okay, Angus. I'll need a little more of an explanation. Help me sort this out. I get that you're full of some righteous indignation over something, but I'm really not sure why you're so pissed."

"I'm pissed"—he rolled his eyes—"because I had to wait all this time. I had to wait for her to die, so I could get this place, sell it, and get the hell out of here."

"Right, and what were you going to do with Liam?"

"Honestly? I figured his little wifey would have died by now, so that was a plan gone wrong."

At that, his heart froze. "What did you do, Angus?"

"Nothing at all. Just hoping it would all be over before anyone found her."

"Did you hit her?"

"She fell," he said, with a beautiful smile on his face. "She was quite clumsy actually, with her huge stomach and all. I gave her a little nudge." He beamed. "I'm pretty sure she won't remember anything, if it comes to that. Besides, it'll be the rantings of a sick woman."

Kascius stared at his youngest brother, realizing that he didn't really know him at all. "I can't believe that you tried to kill Emily. Or that killing someone, anyone, could be an option to get a different life for yourself."

"If she hadn't married my brother, and, after all those attempts hadn't finally gotten pregnant"—he shrugged—"it wouldn't have been an issue."

"Yet how do you expect to get rid of Liam?"

"Well, obviously I'll kill him, although I was really hoping to make it look as if you did it. As in, you came back, and, in a fit of anger, took out everybody."

"Is that what you think? That I'm some uncontrolled person who, after all my military training, would turn around and kill all my family?"

"Sure. Why not?"

"Because, for starters, I'm not you," Kascius said in a quiet tone, hearing the front door open. He tightened his hand on Beamer's collar. The last thing he wanted was for Beamer to get shot. Or himself for that matter. "What do you need the money for anyway?"

He shrugged. "I got into a tight spot, some trouble with

gambling."

At that moment, it all fell together for Kascius. "Jesus Christ, I knew it. You're involved in the dogfights, aren't you?"

Angus stared at him. "What do you know about dogfights?"

Kascius asked him, "Am I right?"

"So, you're right. Who cares? It's not as if that'll do you any good. You don't know who or what or anything that matters."

"How involved are you?" he asked, staring at his brother with that same anger that was building inside for every other injustice that Kascius had been through. "Have you ever done anything in this world that was legit? Or did you just lie, cheat, and steal your way through life, waiting to cash in with this big plan of yours?"

"Hey, gambling is an age-old, honorable profession. Particularly for second and third sons, the ones who don't get handed everything."

"Right. Especially the ones who don't want to work for a living," Kascius said, with a snort. "Liam has been good to you, Angus."

"Sure, but only because of Mam. And, with her finally gone, I'll get my place and sell it."

"And what? You'll take off in the wind, and nobody will know the difference? Is that it?" He stared at his kid brother in disgust. "Do you think nobody will take notice when Liam dies?"

"Hey, the family is beset by tragedy." He shrugged. "What can I say?"

"I think there's a lot you could say." And Kascius heard another sound, one that made his heart race. To cover the noises, he prodded, "Tell me about the betting on the dogfights."

"Jesus, you're such a bloody bleeding heart. You would never understand gambling."

"I bet Dad didn't either."

"Never told him about it. Now Mam? She didn't like it, but she still kept me supplied with the money to keep it going."

"She paid off your gambling debts?" He was shocked at that, though maybe he shouldn't have been.

"Yep, she did. Whether they knew about it or not, I don't know, and I don't really care."

"I didn't think she had that kind of money."

"She had a hidden bank account," he shared, with a laugh. "Money that she stowed away from Dad even. And the money that was supposed to go to the farm. So I guess it didn't go to the farm. It went to my gambling debts instead. Now I want the rest of it."

Kascius stared at his brother, wondering how two siblings could be so completely different than him, but of course it all came down to the upbringing. "Sorry, Angus, but I won't let you do that."

"Do what?" he asked, waving the gun around. "No way in hell you'll stop me. Remember the gun part?"

"Yeah. Remember the asshole part?" A low deep growl came from Beamer.

"You better call that dog off. Otherwise I'll shoot it, as I did the others."

"The others?"

"Yeah, depending on which dog we liked the best and which ones we don't want. We shoot the ones that we don't want."

"Good Christ, Angus, do you have that little regard for life?"

"They're animals. Remember that part? They're nothing but something to make money off of. This one..." He stopped, glared at Beamer, and frowned. "It looks very familiar."

"Yeah, it's the War Dog I came over here to get. It figures that you would be involved with the losers holding him."

Angus stared at the dog. "What do you mean? This can't be the same one. No way in hell. Those guys are too well hidden." Then he pinched his lips together. "Holy shit."

"Well hidden, but not so well hidden, *huh*?" Staring at his brother, Kascius pushed for more. "Where the hell are the ringleaders?"

"I don't know anything about that."

"Other than you of course."

Angus glared at him, some color draining from his face. "Would I have gambling debts if I was one of the ringleaders?"

"Absolutely. If you're picking and choosing the dogs that get to fight versus those that don't." As he spoke, he kept a wary eye on Beamer. "Angus, that dog will take you down before you have a chance to do anything."

"That's fine. If that's the one, it won't be worth the trouble anyway, so I can shoot it now." He lifted his gun, but Beamer was already in the air.

Beamer headed for his gun arm, and Kascius was already on the move as well. He launched himself at Angus, knocking his brother to the ground, even as Beamer snapped his jaw onto Angus's gun hand and started growling deep in his throat again.

Angus screamed a high-pitched sound that brought Liam and Ainsley racing inside, shock on their faces.

"Call the cops and get them out here quick," Kascius yelled.

They both disappeared; then Liam was back almost instantly.

"She's calling the cops. Can you call off the War Dog?"

"I will, but I want to make sure Angus is secured first. Get some rope."

And, with that, Liam ran out, coming right back with ropes. Together they secured Angus. "This should do it"—Liam stepped back—"but what the hell is going on?"

With that, Kascius ordered Beamer to back down. Beamer looked at him in distress, then started to whine. "It's all good, boy." He cuddled the confused dog gently. "I know this is the guy who shot your friend, and he's been a shithead to you the whole time. I can't let you do more. Otherwise you would get a bullet out of this deal, and, for that, I'm sorry, but we've got him now."

Hearing this, Liam turned to Kascius. "What the hell is going on?"

Shaking his head, Kascius took a deep breath and released it, knowing he needed to be calm. He looked over at Liam. "Yeah, that's not a fraction of it. For starters, he and Mam have been robbing the farm blind since Dad died. Apparently she had some secret bank account that had a lot of funds that were supposed to go to the farm, and instead she's been giving the money to Angus, in part at least, for his gambling debts."

"What?"

"Care to guess who's right in the middle of the dogfighting ring here?" With a disgusted shake of his head,

Kascius sat down, hugging Beamer. The stiffness had left the beautiful animal, and finally he laid down his head in Kascius's lap. "It's okay, boy. Everything will be fine now."

Ainsley came racing back in and looked down at Angus. "Oh my God, his arm. I better take a look at that."

"Yeah," Kascius interrupted, "I'm not too bothered about giving him first aid. We'll let the cops make that decision."

Her gaze widened.

"Yeah, there's a bunch of things we still need to sort out. He's saying Dad was killed, but he didn't kill Mam."

"I didn't, you fucking idiots. Ainsley did. Remember?"

"Except I didn't." She glared at him. "I don't know why the hell you would even say that."

"Because he hated you," Liam explained. "You turned him down, and he never could accept that rejection."

Kascius nodded.

She stared at Angus. "We went out one time, and it was obvious that we weren't meant to have any relationship. We had nothing in common and didn't even like each other, so why the hell would you even care?"

"Because you were proving that my goddamn brother was better." Angus looked over at Liam. "I already told him, so I might as well tell you. You weren't supposed to get the farm on your own. At the end, Dad was changing his mind, thinking that Kascius should get it after all. Mam was getting pissed off and fed up about it. She is the one who killed Dad. She put some of his heart medicine into his coffee and gave him an overdose."

Liam stared at him in shock. "What? Why?"

CHAPTER 10

"OH MY GOD," Ainsley cried out, as she suddenly understood. "That's it. She killed him before he could change his will, before everything went to Kascius, or to Kascius and you, Liam."

"But it would go to Kascius," Angus spat. "Dad had already made the appointment to change everything."

Liam still stared at Angus. "Mam killed Dad?" Kascius's gaze went from one brother to the other. As shockers went, this was a doozy.

"She sure did. She'd had enough of him going soft."

"Then who killed her?" Ainsley frowned. "Wasn't that you, Angus?"

"No, it wasn't me." Then he laughed, cackled really. "But it was somebody close to both of us."

She stared at him, then looked at the others. "I don't get it."

"Yet, it was your medicine that killed her." Angus sneered. "And you're the one who gave it to her."

"I gave her medicine every day," she cried out, bewildered, "but I didn't do anything wrong. I didn't overdose her, if that's what you are saying."

"No, but you had it in your purse sometimes, didn't you?"

"I was trying to find a way to stop Bella from getting

access to it and giving herself the wrong dose. Older people are very fragile when it comes to medication, so we were very careful, and I only kept small quantities in her room. When we needed more, I'd bring it with me in the morning, and, yes, I would carry that with me in my purse. But we all knew that. What are you really getting at?"

"As it turns out, somebody at your home got into your stash. That's what killed Mam. It was only a matter of time."

"Sibel?" Ainsley could only stare in fear. "You're lying. You have to be lying."

"Who do you think suggested it?" he said gleefully. "Your sister wanted to get out of town. She was miserable and bitter. She was pissed about the damn house trapping her here."

Kascius immediately stood up and stepped closer to Ainsley. "We need to talk to your sister."

She turned a bewildered look at him but felt the bile rising up the back of her throat. "Oh my God, she used me to kill Bella? Oh my God. Oh my God."

"We only have Angus's word for it, and we know he's a liar. Did you take the medication bottle home?"

She shook her head. "Not normally. Although maybe, as I was always picking up medications and taking them away, after the doctor changed it." She glanced sideways at Angus. "One day, I thought there was less in the bottle than I thought there should be. I wasn't sure, of course, and wondered if I was being paranoid. But still, I didn't know whether someone had tampered with it or had given her too much or what, so I hid it in a different place. I worried it was Bella herself and didn't want her to be a repeat of my brother."

At that, Angus laughed and laughed, almost hysterically.

She stared at him, then looked over at Liam and Kascius. "I don't think I can do this."

"I don't think we have a choice. We have to get to the bottom of this," Liam stated, walking over to his baby brother and smacking him hard. "Why the hell are you laughing?"

"Because even now, after all this time, Ainsley doesn't have a clue. However, if you think I'm going down alone, you're wrong." He looked over at Ainsley. "Your precious brother? He didn't kill himself. He didn't die of natural causes either. Your sister found out that he planned to leave his share of the house to you. She was outraged and killed him that night, before he had his attorney make the changes. Imagine her surprise when she found out that he'd already done it, and you owned two-thirds. Then she was even more stuck, knowing you had most of the house, which meant you had the control but no cash to buy her out, since you'd been caring for him and hadn't been working. So, Sibel's plans to force a sale and to leave were ruined, and she was trapped living with someone she hated even more."

At that, Ainsley fell against the wall, completely distraught, off balance both physically and emotionally. "Please, no," she whispered in horror. "Not Lanson."

Kascius snatched her into his arms and held her close, with Beamer now standing in front of them, still growling down at Angus.

She peered around Kascius. "Say you're lying," she demanded, but, from the look in Angus's gaze, she knew he wasn't.

"The three deaths—Dad, Lanson, and Mam—did you have anything to do with them?" Kascius demanded.

"You mean, outside of planning them? No, that's all on

Sibel. Mam too." Angus chuckled. "Lovely family we've got here," Angus said, as he struggled to get to his feet.

Beamer growled and lunged forward, causing his brother to fall back down.

"That goddamn dog," Angus shouted. "We've had nothing but a shitstorm ever since he got here. We paid that goddamn American family to bring him over, and then that kid balked at the dog going into dogfighting, so we had a hassle getting the War Dog right off the bat. Then I find out that you're hunting for him. That pissed me off. I know what a fucking bulldog you can be, and I knew you wouldn't let it go. But I did not expect you to find the whole pack of dogs." Angus shook his head. "We've flown under the radar all this time. Then you show up and stumble right into them. Good Christ, that's the only way I've made any money these last ten years."

"What are you talking about?" Liam asked in surprise. "What about your job? Your business?"

"I don't have a job, you moron. Working is for losers. Mam thought that too. She said I was destined for bigger and better things."

"What exactly? You were supposed to get there by gambling?"

"The minute she was dead, the farm is all mine."

"How the hell is that going to happen?" Liam asked in frustration. "Most of it is mine."

"Is it though?" Angus asked.

At that, Kascius stepped in. "He was going to kill you, Liam." Kascius held up Angus's handgun. "His big plan was to kill you and to implicate me or something. I wouldn't put it past him to try and take out Ainsley one way or another as well. Emily too. Angus has gone mad. Emily only became part of his radar when the pregnancy stuck."

At that, Liam stared down at his brother with such hatred that Ainsley cried out, "No!"

Kascius immediately stepped forward. "No," he told Liam, "the cops will take care of him. You don't even know the worst of it yet, but you've got to get a grip before the cops come. I'm sorry to tell you this, but Emily didn't collapse or fall. He pushed her, then left, hoping help would come too late to save her and the baby."

Every ounce of color left Liam's face, and Ainsley's legs failed her. Kascius let her slip to the floor, as he held Liam back from attacking Angus.

Ainsley stared at Angus, wondering at so much evil in one man.

"Let me go," Liam yelled. "Just give me five minutes with this little fucker."

"No, Liam," Kascius ordered. "I get it. You know I understand. You think I don't want that same five minutes after everything he has done to me? We're not giving it to him. We're not giving him the satisfaction."

There was a pounding on the door, and suddenly the room was full of cops.

KASCIUS LOOKED OVER at several of them and noted the one involved with the dogs wasn't here. He quickly pulled out his phone, stepped back with Ainsley under his arm again, the War Dog cowering between the two. When he got the detective on the phone, he quickly explained what had happened.

"Good God almighty," he roared. "What the hell?"

"So, yeah, you need to talk to my baby brother, and you need to do it fast, before he decides he's got another ax to grind for somebody else."

"I'm on my way."

"You'll have to check his bank accounts. Payments were made to and from his bank accounts, I'm sure, and there is some account my mother had that is separate from the farm, but the money should have gone to the farm, so she'd figured out how to skim it off somehow. You also need somebody to pick up Ainsley's sister, Sibel. She's the one who tampered with the extra medicine stored offsite at Ainsley's house, after Ainsley hid the medicine there, suspecting somehow my mother was getting too much. Sibel concentrated the dose, so, when Ainsley took a new bottle over, it was too strong, likely causing Mam's death. So, knowing that the main supply of all the meds were kept at Ainsley's for safety, since my mother could be forgetful, Angus enlisted Sibel to tamper with it."

By the time all the explanations were done, statements taken, and Angus had been taken away in cuffs, the three of them gathered in the kitchen. Kascius put on fresh coffee, as Ainsley and Liam sat at the table, still in shock.

Ainsley looked over at Liam. "I'm so sorry."

He frowned at her. "Why? Because we have shitty siblings?"

She gave him a teary smile. "Yeah, I guess so. I had no idea. I don't know how to excuse Sibel's actions."

"That's what made her the perfect person to do it. And, after she got away with it once, it was probably easier to do it again. Plus Angus had her under his thumb, since he knew about your brother because Sibel told him all about it."

"It also explains why she was such a different person

these last few days. She's really been vile since I was arrested."

"It's hard to digest this situation and the people involved," Kascius said, now serving the coffee and reheating the water for pasta. He put down the plate of hamburger for Beamer, who ate it immediately, then sat back, looking for more, his tail wagging madly. "The bottom line is that neither one of them will escape justice now."

"That's all it was, wasn't it? They were both trying to escape their circumstances," Ainsley said.

Kascius added pasta to the boiling water, while the sauce was warming. "Yes, such as I did in a way. Odd to find out now that Dad was killed to stop him from changing his will back to the way he originally intended it to be. And listen, Liam. Don't you dare lose any sleep over that." They talked quietly, while the pasta cooked.

As Kascius served dinner, Liam said, "I don't even know what to say. Now comes the feeling of betrayal for me because I felt very much as if I had done everything Dad ever wanted me to, and to think he'd made that decision and hadn't even told me that he was considering it? No offense to you."

"No, I get it," Kascius said. "I picture him growing old and having some regrets, but who knows. Plus Mam was just as vile. Who kills their own husband? Yet those were the people we were raised by apparently, but luckily it doesn't define us."

Liam stared at him. "I don't even know what to say."

"Don't say anything. Just pick up that fork and eat something," Kascius replied. "The bottom line is that we all have to keep going. And, while we now know a lot more than we did, we have some ugly days to get through. We'll be in a giant shitstorm for some time to come."

"You mean, the cops' questions and all that?" Ainsley asked, as she twirled pasta with her fork.

Kascius worried about how she would handle the incessant blows. "Yes, the questions and, in many ways, the answers will be hard. To think that Mam killed our father is already a shock, but to think that your brother was killed by your sister, and our mother was killed basically by the combination of your sister and our brother. Plus, that Mam stole from the farm to pay Angus's gambling debts is too much. Jesus, it's a murderous lot we have been living with. And I can't even begin to talk about—" He stopped and looked at Liam, and they all knew Kascius was thinking about Emily and the baby.

Liam, seeing his eldest brother overcome with emotions, took the lead and pointed at the food in front of Ainsley. "You heard the man. No excuses. Let's eat."

She stared down at the food. "God, I'm not the least bit hungry."

With his emotions back in check, Kascius looked gratefully at his brother, feeling closer than ever. He smiled at Ainsley. "It's not about being hungry. It's about fuel in the tank. We all have a lot coming our way. We'll need sustenance to get through it. So, hungry or not, *eat.*" And with that, he too started to eat.

CHAPTER 11

TWO DAYS LATER, Ainsley was still marveling at how right Kascius had been, when he'd said it would get ugly. That was the understatement of the century because, not only had it gotten ugly, it had gotten brutally ugly. Thankfully the neighbors and the local people had rallied around them as much as they could once the initial commotion was over. Everybody seemed to more or less pass it off as bad blood happens in too many families. However, once the media had picked it up, the sensational nature of it all fed what seemed to be an endless stream of ridiculously nasty drama.

The media was all over them, trying to make an even bigger and more sensational story out of it. Not that there was any need to make it a bigger story. Her sister had been picked up and had instantly started talking, admitting that, ever since she'd taken down her own brother, she'd felt guilty as hell. Yet not as bad as it got after she had switched up the medicine for Bella, admitting she'd a hand in killing Bella as well.

Sibel did say that her brother had wanted to die, and that made it a mercy killing, but Bella hadn't been quite so ready, and apparently that was in the journals, bits and pieces of it anyway. Yet, when Kascius got the chance to see part of the journals, nothing was there but the ramblings of a disorganized mind, nearing the end of life. He told Ainsley as much, and she had seen the pages that she'd been allowed to see, but nothing made sense.

The recording Kascius had captured on his phone was a key component to solving three murders, and ultimately both Angus and Sibel confessed to their roles in the multiple murders. Therefore, the court proceedings would be much easier than they could have been, though nothing was easy about any of it. Still, the rest of them were all were grateful for that.

Beamer had been the sweetest thing, even during the time Angus was still here. Once the cops took Angus away, Beamer had reverted to being a wonderful relaxed animal. Ainsley certainly understood Kascius wanting to keep him. Kascius had done so well for himself, even with his family largely against him, whereas Ainsley felt that everything over the last five years or more seemed to be such a lie.

Ainsley had basically lived in her robe these last two days. When the doorbell rang, she groaned, as she got up and checked the peephole. Instead of more media, it was Kascius and Beamer and Mistress in tow. She opened the door and looked at him, with a quizzical expression. "Hey, what's up?" She crouched to speak to both dogs. It was her first meeting with Mistress, but the dog was all over her. "She looks great," Ainsley said, examining the healing wound.

"We need to talk."

She led the way to her couch, both dogs jumping up for more cuddles. She winced. "Are you sure? I don't know if I can take in any more." She waved at the big armchair. "You might as well sit, but I warn you that I can't take more bad news."

He smiled at her. "Maybe not, but Emily sent me over

to try and get to the bottom of what's going on."

"What are you talking about? What else could possibly be going on? Although to know the three of them are home together is worth so much."

He laughed. "I don't think any of us are handling this well. We're all still in shock."

"Yeah, you're not kidding, and the media attention has been brutal."

"I was glad to see that you checked the peephole."

"Are you kidding? No way I'll get cornered like that. Can you imagine my picture in the tabloids?" She pointed at her bathrobe, then got up and walked into the kitchen and poured him a coffee.

"I'm glad to see you still have your sense of humor." Looking around, he asked, "Have you decided what you'll do with the house?"

"The house?" she repeated, with a shake of her head. "I have no idea what I'm supposed to do with the house. One-third of it is legally my sister's. However, she'll have a jail cell now, where she'll stay for a good long time. I never realized how much she wanted to sell the place. She did mention it a couple times, but I always shut her down because this was our childhood home. Coming back every day from working with Bella, it really was a sanctuary for me."

"And now?"

"I've already contacted a Realtor to see what we can do about selling it."

He nodded. "Doesn't quite have the same memories anymore, I'll bet."

"No. To know that my brother died here at her hand, especially after I was suspicious that he had committed suicide? I never once considered she'd murdered him. Now it all is just too much to contemplate."

"It threw me for a loop too." He smiled, then looked at the mug of coffee in his hand and back up at her. "So, what about us?"

She shifted on the couch, studying him carefully. "What? I didn't think there was an *us*."

"According to Liam, he was told you were marrying Angus but finally figured out it was all lies. Nobody ever cleared that up for me. I thought the right thing to do would be to stay away. Then you two could make a decent life, without me showing up and rocking the boat."

She sagged deeper into the couch. "Is that why you didn't come home?"

"No, not really. It just it made it easier."

She nodded slowly. "I guess I can understand that, but I don't know why you're bringing it up now. That was a long time ago."

"I'm bringing it up now because, in all this time, you haven't found anybody, right?"

"Nope," she admitted, "but I had a lot going on. Besides, what difference does that make?"

"The thing is, I'm hoping maybe you changed your mind on some things, but, if not, I need to know."

"Okay, but I still really don't know what you're talking about." She stared at him in confusion.

"You were always adamantly against all those injuries that military men, like your brother, had."

"Well, yeah, they were a constant source of trouble for Lanson, and he could never quite heal. He was in a lot of pain." She frowned, wondering where he was going with this.

"If I remember right, you said you would never sign up

to be around somebody dealing with a disability."

At that, her brain snapped to attention, and she realized this must be what Liam had been talking about. "I was also very emotional and upset over the loss of my brother at the time, so I can't say that's something I would want to be held to now. Plus I'm a nurse, and I know an awful lot more now."

"So, that's not how you feel then?"

"No, that's not how I feel. Why do you ask?"

"Because I have a disability of my own. It's something that's fairly visible, though, according to Liam, you had no idea."

"Oh, so he told you that, did he?" She winced. "I'm still in the dark and have no idea what disability you're talking about. You've got four limbs and look fine. You can see and hear, so what's left? Catheter? Colostomy bag? What? I really don't know."

He laughed. "Thankfully no. All my bodily functions are still intact, but ..." He reached down, kicked off his boot, and lifted his pants leg.

Suddenly she was staring at a prosthetic. She swallowed hard and nodded. "That's ... very similar to Lanson's."

"Except for one thing. Mine has healed fully," he noted, and he pointed to an area above the knee joint. "It stops here."

"And you're showing me this why?" She still stared at the leg, thinking of all the things that Lanson had suffered from.

"Because I still care about you," Kascius said calmly. "I've decided that I'm not going to beat around the bush anymore. So I want to know if you still have any feelings for me and if this leg is a deal breaker?"

She looked back and forth between his leg and his face. "You still care?" That was the only thing she could grasp out of any of it.

He chuckled. "Yeah, I do. And Angus seemed to think that you still cared, at least that's what I got out of something I heard him say. However, it's quite possible that he was caught up in his own nasty mind and didn't know what he was talking about."

"Oh, I still care." She looked him directly in the eye. "I figured there was no way in hell that you did."

"I do," he said gently. "Very much. Does that mean you would be interested in seeing what we still might have, with a fresh start?"

She frowned. "Does that mean you're staying? Because, if there's anything all this has taught me, it is that I'm not sure I'm cut out for a long-distance relationship. Hell, I couldn't even keep a decent relationship with my sister, who lived in the same house with me."

"Now that's not fair. That was her problem, not yours."

"Doesn't feel like it," she muttered.

He nodded. "It'll take a long time for all of us to heal, but it will happen. I'm not expecting it to be overnight. And you're evading the evident question here."

"No, I'm not. Not really. I'm a little in shock that you even need to ask. There's never been anyone else for me. You know that, right?"

He shook his head. "No, I don't know that at all. After we lost Lanson, I wasn't sure what to think. I assumed you would turn to me for comfort, but it seemed to be the opposite, as if I made it worse or something."

"I probably would have turned to you, except I didn't even really know how to grieve. And I was full of suspicion that Lanson had killed himself, and that made me feel terribly guilty and angry."

"So, you didn't think I'd killed him?" he asked cautiously.

She shook her head. "No, I never thought that. Oh my God, that's what you thought, isn't it?"

"I added that to everything else that was going on in my world at the time."

"I can't believe what a nightmare your family turned out to be." Then she gave a broken laugh. "Then look at mine."

"That's partly why I'm here, but again you're still not answering my question."

She got up, walked over, and climbed into his lap. His arms immediately wrapped around her—no hesitation, just a wonderful sense of homecoming. "The answer is absolutely I totally still care and never stopped." She cuddled him close. "I thought my life would be lonely, that I would grow old alone, with no one to come home to because you had chosen a life far away, instead of here with me."

"I had to get away from rejection on all sides," Kascius explained, as he reached up a palm to her cheek. "It was destroying me. And, as much as you tell yourself that having your parents hate your guts doesn't matter, it does. It matters a lot," he said gently. "I thought I'd dealt with it, and sometimes I think I really have, but then it all comes back up again."

"Yeah. That'll be all of us for a while."

"Yeah, it will." He hugged her tight. "But it doesn't have to be our future, and I would like nothing better than to start fresh."

"You mean, we go back to where we were?" she asked hesitantly.

"Nope, really start fresh. I don't want to go back to what we had before. I want something better. We're both different people now. We're older, more mature. I want to start with better communication and a commitment to being honest with each other, but it all depends on you."

She looked up at him and smiled. "Not really, it's on both of us."

"Oh, and the dogs are part of the package too."

"What about the dogs?" she asked.

"I'm keeping them, both of them. I plan to take them both home to the farm, but I'm also checking out how you feel about having dogs in my life."

"I love Beamer already, and Mistress is adorable." Hearing her name, Mistress barked, then stretched out on the couch.

"I'm thinking about doing dog training for real." Then he explained what the detective had suggested.

"Wow, and law enforcement is where you belong, isn't it?"

"Yes and no. I'm guessing my leg would keep me from getting cleared for full duty, and I'm not a halfway kind of guy, you know? So, I'm looking at pursuing the dog training angle instead. With my military credentials, I could always consult with the cops, if they needed help with something. Yet I like the idea of doing my own thing with K9 training. Possibly therapy animals are an option too. It's a little more positive, you know?"

"Yeah. I would love that, and, if it keeps you here, I would love it even more." Then she looped her arms around his neck and kissed him on the cheek. "God, I'm so glad you came home."

"Me too. So, if nothing else, you owe Beamer here a big

thank you."

She chuckled and looked at the big dog, standing in the living room, looking back at her. He barked once, wagging his tail. Smiling, she clambered off Kascius's lap, walked over, and dropped to her knees, hugging Beamer. "You know I've always loved dogs."

"Yeah, but you used to love me too, and that changed."

"It never changed," she clarified. "I was just a crazy mixed-up fool."

"We both had some growing up to do."

Beamer nudged her with his head, and she gently gave him a head scratch. "He's a big baby, isn't he? Not so ferocious now, are you, boy?"

"He's looking for a home. A home where he doesn't have to get shuffled around anymore. And he definitely doesn't want to get anywhere near a dogfighting ring."

"Speaking of that, what will the authorities do with all those dogs?"

"I don't know, but I want to take on as many as I can. I've teamed up with a vet to see what kind of training they've had and to sort out what disposition we're dealing with at this point. Some of them, the real seasoned fighters, may have to be put down, but for the rest? Well, I've already talked to Liam about using a few acres for pens."

She chuckled. "I don't think he'd have a problem with that."

"I think he's thrilled that I'm looking at staying home, and I think he's a little worried that I want the farm."

"Especially after finding out what happened with your father changing his mind."

"I think we'll come to an agreement on that, and I'll take a few acres and build a house," he shared.

She frowned. "You have that kind of money?"

"I do," he said, with a smile. "I didn't have anybody to spend it on all these years, and I was very well paid. Plus I think Liam wants to help out some, at least with labor and equipment, as much as he can. So, I think I can do it, as long as you're interested."

"Interested?" she whispered, dazed at the rapid turn of events, as she moved towards him. "I'm not sure what you're asking, but obviously I'm interested in seeing what we can do for a relationship."

"I was hoping that we could skip a few steps and maybe go right to the part where you show me undivided devotion and trust."

She looked at him in joy. "Oh, I'm already there. I always have been."

He pulled her chin down close to him and whispered, "It's a good thing because that house I'm building is for the two of us. I don't want to waste any more time. Life is too short, too convoluted, and too full of shit sometimes. I'm really hoping we can skip ahead and go straight to the good stuff."

And, with that, she noted one of his hands were already underneath her robe and up against her waist. She started to laugh. "Uh, what kind of good stuff are you looking for?" she asked in a teasing voice.

"Anything and everything you've got to give." He grinned broadly, just before he kissed her deeply.

When she finally pulled back, she stared down at him. "You do know I never wanted anything else, right?"

"I was hoping that maybe that was true but never really let myself believe it. But now, after what we've all been through, I figured I would jump right into our future."

"What we have is what we should have had years ago." She looped her arms around his neck. "Each other is really all we need." And this time she bent her head and kissed him.

Kascius quickly snagged her tighter in his arms and carried her upstairs. Ainsley laughed and then cried out, "Your leg, you'll break our necks on these stairs."

"As I've said, I'm healed, and I'm just fine."

She looked at him in amazement. "Seriously?"

"Yeah, it's fine and very functional. It just doesn't look that pretty."

"I don't care about that. The fact that you're home and even talking to me is absolutely amazing, and I want to thank you for coming home, and I'll probably say it one thousand times."

"You can always show me instead." He gave a wicked waggle of his eyebrows. As he laid her on the bed, he eyed her tiny camisole and panties, now revealed when the robe opened up.

She hopped up, peeled off the robe, and stared at him. "One of us is wearing way-too-many clothes."

He cocked his head to the side. "Maybe you better do something about that."

Immediately her hands reached for his belt buckle, and she laughed. "God, I missed this, missed you, missed the sex, the laughter, the cuddling, all of it."

"Totally without it?" he asked.

"Yeah, totally without it. I looked around a little from time to time, but the men I saw? They just weren't you." She said it so simply and so honestly that he felt his heart swell with emotions as he felt love, something that had been lacking in his life. He brushed away her hands and stepped out of his clothes in a heartbeat, and then realized it was the first that she'd fully seen his prosthetic.

She reached out a hand and touched his leg. "I'm really sorry I wasn't there to help you get through this, but, at the same time, it would have broken me to see you so hurt."

"We've both made it through some tough times, so don't worry about it. I really am okay."

"Even if you're not, you'll let me know if it's a problem, won't you?" she asked.

"We'll see," he whispered, with a big grin. "So, do you want it off or on?"

"I don't have time for you to take it off," she said, as she pulled her camisole over her head. As she went to step out of her panties, he stopped her.

"Let me," he offered, with a smoky passion in his voice.

She laid down on the bed and opened her arms, feeling that same old awareness she had felt so long ago. When his hands reached for her, and his lips, she came unglued. "Christ, as soon as I open the floodgates, that same heat and passion is here, just like before," she cried out, already twisting under his hands. "Why didn't you come home years ago?"

He laughed, as he bent over and took one nipple deep into his mouth, teasing it with his tongue, before slowly moving to the other one. "I'm here now," he whispered, as he placed a few kisses along her shoulder and down to the soft skin of her arm and down to her elbow. His fingers gently massaged her breasts and all the way down to her hip bones and her flat belly.

"Christ." She pulled him up and whispered, "You know

it'll take a few times to get through this initial rush, right?"

"I do." He gently slid his fingers into the soft folds of flesh between her legs and stroked the moisture up and around, before sliding up her body. He leaned over and kissed one nipple, laving it with his hot tongue.

She twisted beneath him, her hands running all over his body, stopping at one particularly long welt. "You have even more scars."

"It doesn't matter because I'm here, and I'm whole. What I really am is excited to be one with you, as long as we can."

"How about a lifetime?" she whispered, pulling him closer into her arms.

"Suits me," he whispered back. He slowly positioned himself, but she wasn't having any of that.

She wrapped her thighs high on his hips and surged upward, impaling herself on his shaft.

He groaned as he sank deeper, pressing himself as far as he could go.

She twisted beneath him, crying out, "Christ." She arched up, chanting his name. He laughed and started to move.

When she came apart in his arms, he bowed his head, holding her, trying to feel every ripple and shiver in her body. He cherished every moment of her joy and her passion, and then, when he couldn't stand anymore, he plunged into her body, holding her hips hard, as he moved deeper and faster.

When she came apart a second time, it was magical. He groaned and quickly joined her on the other side. He collapsed beside her, watching her tears stream down her face.

"Oh my God." He rose onto an elbow. "Did I hurt you?"

She shook her head, looped her arms around his neck, pulled him down, and whispered, "Yes. By staying away for so long. This was all I ever wanted."

"What, sex?" he asked in a teasing voice.

She smacked him lightly on the hip. "No. You. It's all about you."

"Now we have the rest of our lives to share. We'll build a house and build a future for ourselves." He kissed her gently on the temple. "Personally, I didn't think I would ever have that in my life, so I am really grateful that I came home and that you were waiting for me."

She looped a leg around his hip, pulling him back atop her. "Home is exactly where you belong." And, with that, she wrapped her arms around his neck and kissed him again.

EPILOGUE

Kat looked at Badger, as he hung up the phone. "Good God. Even listening in on Speakerphone, I have to ask. What the hell was that all about?"

"One very convoluted dog story."

"Are there going to be charges for everybody?" she asked, looking at her husband in wonder. "It's hard to even sort out who did what because so many angles are involved."

"There will definitely be a lot of charges. I've already contacted the war department about the family who knowingly sold a War Dog into a dogfighting ring over in Scotland. They're assessing what options they have, and they've been talking to the Scottish authorities as well. I would think the family will be prevented from adopting pets, at least for a time, but they also aided and abetted a dogfighting ring, and that is a crime over there, so they aren't getting away free and clear by any means."

"I can't believe all those murders." Kat stared at her husband. "Such little regard for life."

"That is stunning and over how many years? A decade? Just amazing. Both of Kascius's parents, and nearly his brother and sister-in-law and their baby, plus Ainsley's brother too. It's a miracle there weren't several more murders."

"Kascius did say the plan evolved as needed, but, at one

point, they would all be killed by Angus, so he could get the whole farm and sell it. How did he think he would get away with that?" Kat cried out.

"One of his early plans was to knock out Kascius, making it seem as if Kascius had killed Liam and the rest of them, before he killed himself—all in some angry PTSD event. But I think, in the heat of the moment, once it all came down, everyone was just reacting."

"It's all so crazy. My God. You know I'm half scared to pick the next case after this one." She sat back and looked at Badger. "Yet some of these case files are pretty compelling."

"Here I was thinking that tracking down a dog and taking it back to the family or finding another family would be all there was to it, but some of these cases end up pretty convoluted and dangerous as hell."

A cough at the doorway had Kat looking up and smiling. "Hey, Timber. How are you?"

The huge tree of a man sported a tinge of silver in his hair to match the blue-metal prosthetic on his right leg. He shrugged. "I'm fine. As always."

"Which means you're holding but not fine," Kat pointed out.

His gaze narrowed, and his lips twitched. "Blunt, aren't you?"

"To the point, you mean." She didn't back down. Timber had been in and out of the Titanium Corp office for a good six months now. He was one hell of a carpenter and a handyman, had been a hell of a Navy SEAL, and now wanted little to do with anyone. He was polite and respectful but a loner. Some of the men here were friendly, happy to go with others for a beer, a walk, or just to sit around, enjoy a BBQ. Every time Timber was invited, he refused.

"What do you need?" Badger asked the new arrival.

Timber hesitated. "There's a few acres one mile or two from here …"

"Around Gando's Pond?"

Timber nodded. "Yeah. I wonder if you know who owns it?"

Badger looked at Kat, who stared back at him. "You know Killerman, right?" she suggested to her husband.

Badger nodded. "Andy Killerman. He's got a place close to it. Why?"

Kat watched Timber wrestle whether to share or not. Finally he shrugged. "I was wondering if it's for sale."

"It's a great place, if you could get it," Kat said warmly. "We have often looked at it and wondered."

Timber nodded. "I'll talk to Andy."

"Do you know him?" Kat was surprised. Timber never seemed to speak to the others. So knowing someone outside of this group here was surprising.

"No, but I will." With that, Timber walked back out.

Badger looked over at Kat. "What was that all about?"

Her laughter rang free. "I'd say he's looking to settle close by but not too close."

Surprised, Badger nodded. "He's a hell of a good guy. But that piece is what? Twenty acres? It won't come cheap."

"I think it's closer to thirty acres. Yet wooded and pastured, with a creek backing onto Gando's Pond itself. If Timber can get it, that would be a hell of a coup. But what would he do with it?"

The two looked at each other. "Does he like dogs?" Badger asked, with a grin. "Our War Dog files will dwindle down eventually, as we near the end of the requests from the war department. Yet, as we both know, there is a hell of a need out there for someone to help out these animals in other ways."

Hearing a bark, both Badger and Kat turned to look out the window. And watched as a dog raced toward Timber. He bent down to greet it, his face lighting with joy. Too soon the dog was called back by its owner. Kat turned to Badger. "Well, that answered that question."

"Yeah, but I'm not sure Timber's ready yet to be a full-time dog owner."

"No, not yet. Timber is still a mystery I've been trying to understand for months."

"You and me both. Not to mention the rest of the team is also curious about Timber."

Kat added, "But back to today's issue. What else do we have for cases?"

Badger looked down at the file he had chosen next. "I don't know what to do about this one either."

"What's the matter?" she asked.

"There's a woman doing animal therapy and training, who says she ended up with a War Dog and has no idea how she got it."

Kat frowned at him. "That's a twist."

"It is. She has provided the registration number, and it fits a War Dog that went missing."

"So, what's the problem? Case closed, right?"

"Somebody still needs to go do a welfare check on the dog, and honestly she sounded really nervous on the phone. Maybe something is deeper there than it appears on the surface."

"Nervous how?"

"I'm not sure, but I've got somebody in mind for this one. Do you remember Declan?"

She frowned at Badger. "Declan was going to come work for us but then went in for more surgery or something, wasn't it?"

Her husband nodded. "Yeah, he was in a friendly fire incident that took out his leg, a couple ribs, and also broke his collarbone."

"That doesn't sound so friendly," she said in disgust.

"I know, but he lives in the same state as the animal therapist, so it seems to be a good fit for him. I was thinking about giving him a call to see if he's up for helping out a little damsel in distress."

Her eyes widened. "Do we really think this is a damsel in distress?"

Badger shrugged. "All I can tell you is that she sounded really nervous on the phone."

"Well, hell, let's do it then."

With that, Badger reached for the phone, again putting it on Speakerphone. "Declan, Badger and Kat here. So, do you want to be a hero?"

Declan laughed. "Always. What do you need?"

This concludes Book 20 of The K9 Files: Kascius.
Read about Declan: The K9 Files, Book 21

THE K9 FILES: DECLAN (BOOK #21)

Welcome to the all new K9 Files series reconnecting readers with the unforgettable men from SEALs of Steel in a new series of action packed, page turning romantic suspense that fans have come to expect from USA TODAY Bestselling author Dale Mayer. Pssst... you'll meet other favorite characters from SEALs of Honor and Heroes for Hire too!

Doing a wellness check on a War Dog—now in the care of a woman who trains therapy dogs—Declan sees the aftermath of an attack. The trainer hopes for some assistance in how to work with the War Dog, Shelby, but apparently someone didn't want Carly working with Shelby at all. Or was the attack connected to something else in Carly's past?

Carly has been through enough heartache for a lifetime. Her parents were murdered a few years back, leaving her alone in the world; even worse, the case was never solved, leaving her stuck in the past. She'd done her best to move on, ... but this attack brings it all back.

The situation goes from bad to worse, as yet another attack involves an old friend, as he tries to explain something about her parents' case to her. It's hard for Carly to believe, but is it possible that the attacks on her connect to her parents' murders? From Declan's point of view, how can it not?

Find Book 21 here!

To find out more visit Dale Mayer's website.

https://geni.us/DMSDeclan

Author's Note

Thank you for reading Kascius: The K9 Files, Book 20! If you enjoyed the book, please take a moment and leave a short review.

Dear reader,

I love to hear from readers, and you can contact me at my website: www.dalemayer.com or at my Facebook author page. To be informed of new releases and special offers, sign up for my newsletter or follow me on BookBub. And if you are interested in joining Dale Mayer's Reader Group, here is the Facebook sign up page.
http://geni.us/DaleMayerFBGroup

Cheers,
Dale Mayer

Get THREE Free Books Now!

Have you met the SEALS of Honor?

SEALs of Honor Books 1, 2, and 3. Follow the stories of brave, badass warriors who serve their country with honor and love their women to the limits of life and death.

Read Mason, Hawk, and Dane right now for FREE.

Go here and tell me where to send them!
https://dalemayer.com/masonfree/

About the Author

Dale Mayer is a *USA Today* best-selling author, best known for her SEALs military romances, her Psychic Visions series, and her Lovely Lethal Garden cozy series. Her contemporary romances are raw and full of passion and emotion (Broken But ... Mending, Hathaway House series). Her thrillers will keep you guessing (Kate Morgan, By Death series), and her romantic comedies will keep you giggling (*It's a Dog's Life*, a stand-alone novella; and the Broken Protocols series, starring Charming Marvin, the cat).

Dale honors the stories that come to her—and some of them are crazy, break all the rules and cross multiple genres!

To go with her fiction, she also writes nonfiction in many different fields, with books available on résumé writing, companion gardening, and the US mortgage system. All her books are available in print and ebook format.

Connect with Dale Mayer Online

Dale's Website – www.dalemayer.com
Twitter – @DaleMayer
Facebook Page – geni.us/DaleMayerFBFanPage
Facebook Group – geni.us/DaleMayerFBGroup
BookBub – geni.us/DaleMayerBookbub
Instagram – geni.us/DaleMayerInstagram
Goodreads – geni.us/DaleMayerGoodreads
Newsletter – geni.us/DaleNews

Also by Dale Mayer

Published Adult Books:

Shadow Recon
Magnus, Book 1
Rogan, Book 2
Egan, Book 3
Barret, Book 4

Bullard's Battle
Ryland's Reach, Book 1
Cain's Cross, Book 2
Eton's Escape, Book 3
Garret's Gambit, Book 4
Kano's Keep, Book 5
Fallon's Flaw, Book 6
Quinn's Quest, Book 7
Bullard's Beauty, Book 8
Bullard's Best, Book 9
Bullard's Battle, Books 1–2
Bullard's Battle, Books 3–4
Bullard's Battle, Books 5–6
Bullard's Battle, Books 7–8

Terkel's Team
Damon's Deal, Book 1
Wade's War, Book 2

Gage's Goal, Book 3
Calum's Contact, Book 4
Rick's Road, Book 5
Scott's Summit, Book 6
Brody's Beast, Book 7
Terkel's Twist, Book 8
Terkel's Triumph, Book 9

Terkel's Guardian
Radar, Book 1

Kate Morgan
Simon Says… Hide, Book 1
Simon Says… Jump, Book 2
Simon Says… Ride, Book 3
Simon Says… Scream, Book 4
Simon Says… Run, Book 5
Simon Says… Walk, Book 6
Simon Says… Forgive, Book 7

Hathaway House
Aaron, Book 1
Brock, Book 2
Cole, Book 3
Denton, Book 4
Elliot, Book 5
Finn, Book 6
Gregory, Book 7
Heath, Book 8
Iain, Book 9
Jaden, Book 10
Keith, Book 11

Lance, Book 12
Melissa, Book 13
Nash, Book 14
Owen, Book 15
Percy, Book 16
Quinton, Book 17
Ryatt, Book 18
Spencer, Book 19
Timothy, Book 20
Hathaway House, Books 1–3
Hathaway House, Books 4–6
Hathaway House, Books 7–9

The K9 Files
Ethan, Book 1
Pierce, Book 2
Zane, Book 3
Blaze, Book 4
Lucas, Book 5
Parker, Book 6
Carter, Book 7
Weston, Book 8
Greyson, Book 9
Rowan, Book 10
Caleb, Book 11
Kurt, Book 12
Tucker, Book 13
Harley, Book 14
Kyron, Book 15
Jenner, Book 16
Rhys, Book 17
Landon, Book 18

Harper, Book 19
Kascius, Book 20
Declan, Book 21
The K9 Files, Books 1–2
The K9 Files, Books 3–4
The K9 Files, Books 5–6
The K9 Files, Books 7–8
The K9 Files, Books 9–10
The K9 Files, Books 11–12

Lovely Lethal Gardens
Arsenic in the Azaleas, Book 1
Bones in the Begonias, Book 2
Corpse in the Carnations, Book 3
Daggers in the Dahlias, Book 4
Evidence in the Echinacea, Book 5
Footprints in the Ferns, Book 6
Gun in the Gardenias, Book 7
Handcuffs in the Heather, Book 8
Ice Pick in the Ivy, Book 9
Jewels in the Juniper, Book 10
Killer in the Kiwis, Book 11
Lifeless in the Lilies, Book 12
Murder in the Marigolds, Book 13
Nabbed in the Nasturtiums, Book 14
Offed in the Orchids, Book 15
Poison in the Pansies, Book 16
Quarry in the Quince, Book 17
Revenge in the Roses, Book 18
Silenced in the Sunflowers, Book 19
Toes up in the Tulips, Book 20
Uzi in the Urn, Book 21

Victim in the Violets, Book 22
Lovely Lethal Gardens, Books 1–2
Lovely Lethal Gardens, Books 3–4
Lovely Lethal Gardens, Books 5–6
Lovely Lethal Gardens, Books 7–8
Lovely Lethal Gardens, Books 9–10

Psychic Visions Series
Tuesday's Child
Hide 'n Go Seek
Maddy's Floor
Garden of Sorrow
Knock Knock…
Rare Find
Eyes to the Soul
Now You See Her
Shattered
Into the Abyss
Seeds of Malice
Eye of the Falcon
Itsy-Bitsy Spider
Unmasked
Deep Beneath
From the Ashes
Stroke of Death
Ice Maiden
Snap, Crackle…
What If…
Talking Bones
String of Tears
Inked Forever
Psychic Visions Books 1–3

Psychic Visions Books 4–6
Psychic Visions Books 7–9

By Death Series
Touched by Death
Haunted by Death
Chilled by Death
By Death Books 1–3

Broken Protocols – Romantic Comedy Series
Cat's Meow
Cat's Pajamas
Cat's Cradle
Cat's Claus
Broken Protocols 1-4

Broken and... Mending
Skin
Scars
Scales (of Justice)
Broken but… Mending 1-3

Glory
Genesis
Tori
Celeste
Glory Trilogy

Biker Blues
Morgan: Biker Blues, Volume 1
Cash: Biker Blues, Volume 2

SEALs of Honor

Mason: SEALs of Honor, Book 1
Hawk: SEALs of Honor, Book 2
Dane: SEALs of Honor, Book 3
Swede: SEALs of Honor, Book 4
Shadow: SEALs of Honor, Book 5
Cooper: SEALs of Honor, Book 6
Markus: SEALs of Honor, Book 7
Evan: SEALs of Honor, Book 8
Mason's Wish: SEALs of Honor, Book 9
Chase: SEALs of Honor, Book 10
Brett: SEALs of Honor, Book 11
Devlin: SEALs of Honor, Book 12
Easton: SEALs of Honor, Book 13
Ryder: SEALs of Honor, Book 14
Macklin: SEALs of Honor, Book 15
Corey: SEALs of Honor, Book 16
Warrick: SEALs of Honor, Book 17
Tanner: SEALs of Honor, Book 18
Jackson: SEALs of Honor, Book 19
Kanen: SEALs of Honor, Book 20
Nelson: SEALs of Honor, Book 21
Taylor: SEALs of Honor, Book 22
Colton: SEALs of Honor, Book 23
Troy: SEALs of Honor, Book 24
Axel: SEALs of Honor, Book 25
Baylor: SEALs of Honor, Book 26
Hudson: SEALs of Honor, Book 27
Lachlan: SEALs of Honor, Book 28
Paxton: SEALs of Honor, Book 29
Bronson: SEALs of Honor, Book 30
Hale: SEALs of Honor, Book 31

SEALs of Honor, Books 1–3
SEALs of Honor, Books 4–6
SEALs of Honor, Books 7–10
SEALs of Honor, Books 11–13
SEALs of Honor, Books 14–16
SEALs of Honor, Books 17–19
SEALs of Honor, Books 20–22
SEALs of Honor, Books 23–25

Heroes for Hire
Levi's Legend: Heroes for Hire, Book 1
Stone's Surrender: Heroes for Hire, Book 2
Merk's Mistake: Heroes for Hire, Book 3
Rhodes's Reward: Heroes for Hire, Book 4
Flynn's Firecracker: Heroes for Hire, Book 5
Logan's Light: Heroes for Hire, Book 6
Harrison's Heart: Heroes for Hire, Book 7
Saul's Sweetheart: Heroes for Hire, Book 8
Dakota's Delight: Heroes for Hire, Book 9
Tyson's Treasure: Heroes for Hire, Book 10
Jace's Jewel: Heroes for Hire, Book 11
Rory's Rose: Heroes for Hire, Book 12
Brandon's Bliss: Heroes for Hire, Book 13
Liam's Lily: Heroes for Hire, Book 14
North's Nikki: Heroes for Hire, Book 15
Anders's Angel: Heroes for Hire, Book 16
Reyes's Raina: Heroes for Hire, Book 17
Dezi's Diamond: Heroes for Hire, Book 18
Vince's Vixen: Heroes for Hire, Book 19
Ice's Icing: Heroes for Hire, Book 20
Johan's Joy: Heroes for Hire, Book 21
Galen's Gemma: Heroes for Hire, Book 22

Zack's Zest: Heroes for Hire, Book 23
Bonaparte's Belle: Heroes for Hire, Book 24
Noah's Nemesis: Heroes for Hire, Book 25
Tomas's Trials: Heroes for Hire, Book 26
Carson's Choice: Heroes for Hire, Book 27
Dante's Decision: Heroes for Hire, Book 28
Steve's Solace: Heroes for Hire, Book 29
Heroes for Hire, Books 1–3
Heroes for Hire, Books 4–6
Heroes for Hire, Books 7–9
Heroes for Hire, Books 10–12
Heroes for Hire, Books 13–15
Heroes for Hire, Books 16–18
Heroes for Hire, Books 19–21
Heroes for Hire, Books 22–24

SEALs of Steel
Badger: SEALs of Steel, Book 1
Erick: SEALs of Steel, Book 2
Cade: SEALs of Steel, Book 3
Talon: SEALs of Steel, Book 4
Laszlo: SEALs of Steel, Book 5
Geir: SEALs of Steel, Book 6
Jager: SEALs of Steel, Book 7
The Final Reveal: SEALs of Steel, Book 8
SEALs of Steel, Books 1–4
SEALs of Steel, Books 5–8
SEALs of Steel, Books 1–8

The Mavericks
Kerrick, Book 1
Griffin, Book 2

Jax, Book 3
Beau, Book 4
Asher, Book 5
Ryker, Book 6
Miles, Book 7
Nico, Book 8
Keane, Book 9
Lennox, Book 10
Gavin, Book 11
Shane, Book 12
Diesel, Book 13
Jerricho, Book 14
Killian, Book 15
Hatch, Book 16
Corbin, Book 17
Aiden, Book 18
The Mavericks, Books 1–2
The Mavericks, Books 3–4
The Mavericks, Books 5–6
The Mavericks, Books 7–8
The Mavericks, Books 9–10
The Mavericks, Books 11–12

Standalone Novellas
It's a Dog's Life
Riana's Revenge
Second Chances

Published Young Adult Books:

Family Blood Ties Series
Vampire in Denial

Vampire in Distress
Vampire in Design
Vampire in Deceit
Vampire in Defiance
Vampire in Conflict
Vampire in Chaos
Vampire in Crisis
Vampire in Control
Vampire in Charge
Family Blood Ties Set 1–3
Family Blood Ties Set 1–5
Family Blood Ties Set 4–6
Family Blood Ties Set 7–9
Sian's Solution, A Family Blood Ties Series Prequel Novelette

Design series
Dangerous Designs
Deadly Designs
Darkest Designs
Design Series Trilogy

Standalone
In Cassie's Corner
Gem Stone (a Gemma Stone Mystery)
Time Thieves

Published Non-Fiction Books:

Career Essentials
Career Essentials: The Résumé
Career Essentials: The Cover Letter
Career Essentials: The Interview
Career Essentials: 3 in 1

Made in the USA
Monee, IL
27 May 2023